RANGER PROTECTION

TEXAS RANGER HEROES

LYNN SHANNON

RANGER PROTECTION

For my husband and children.
You believed in my dream as much as I did. My success is
our success. I couldn't have done it without you.

I sought the Lord, and he answered me;
he delivered me from all my fears.

PSALM 34:4

ONE

A high-pitched wail reverberated through the grocery store, loud enough to shatter glass.

Tara winced. She tried rocking the shopping cart, but seven-month-old Maddy had no patience when she was hungry and tired. The baby's body was rigid in the car seat carrier hooked to the front of the shopping cart. Her puckered hands formed into fists and her eyes were squeezed shut, tears leaking from the corners. She resembled a furious boxer giving up a war cry.

"Sixty-nine fifty, ma'am." The clerk's brow furrowed. Tara fumbled with her wallet while fishing for the pacifier buried somewhere underneath Maddy. Why hadn't she hooked it to the baby's outfit using the string? Her fingers brushed against the plastic. She yanked it out and wiggled it between Maddy's lips. The baby latched on, her wail replaced with furious sucking.

Tara took the few seconds of reprieve to swipe her credit card across the machine, then shoved her wallet back inside her purse. It rustled against the slew of dry cleaning slips from the last couple of weeks. Another errand left undone. A last-minute patient had arrived at the clinic, setting her entire schedule off-kilter. She'd barely made it in time to pick up Maddy at daycare. The grocery store had been a necessary stop. They'd scraped the bottom of the formula can this morning and she had only three diapers left.

Maddy spit out the pacifier and her chin trembled. Oh, no. Tara wiggled the cart and willed the receipt to print faster. The baby sucked in a deep breath and let loose. Flustered, Tara hastily grabbed the receipt and scooped up the last of the bags from the end of the counter, dumping them into her cart. She rushed out the sliding doors into the cool October night.

Shoot, where was her car? She scanned the parking lot. She'd come in on the right-hand side. Weak spotlights illuminated hulking vehicles. The enticing scent of french fries from the fast-food restaurant across the street tickled her nose, and Tara's stomach rumbled. It was way past dinner time for both of them. She tucked Maddy's blanket around her as she moved to the far side of the parking lot. The loose wheel on the cart wobbled.

"It's going to be fine, honey. Promise. Two minutes and we'll be home."

Her little sedan was hidden in the dark between two SUVs. The overhead light next to her parking spot was out. No wonder she hadn't been able to find her car. Tara dug her keys out of her purse and hit the fob. The trunk swung open.

A piece of paper fluttered across the space between two vehicles. Tara shivered in the chilly wind. She considered putting Maddy in the car, but the baby would only scream, and for the moment she was quiet. Better to load the car first.

Tara grabbed the diapers from the cart and tossed them into the trunk. Her purse strap slid down, and she threw it in as well before turning back to scoop up a couple of canvas sacks. Formula and baby food knocked together. Maddy fussed.

"Sweetheart, please, give me just a minute—"

Glass crunched. The hair on the back of her neck stood up and she spun. A man dressed in black with a ski mask over his face materialized out of the shadows. He lifted his arm, and she was looking down the barrel of a gun.

She froze.

What did he want? Money? Her car? Or—she swallowed hard—did he want something else? From her seat on the cart, Maddy whimpered. The masked man's attention slid to the left. It lingered on the baby and Tara's heart galloped. Her gaze darted around the parking lot, but it was empty.

She backed up half a step, putting herself between the man and Maddy. The shopping cart handle bumped against her back. Tara's breath came in shallow spurts.

"Here." She lifted her car keys. Her hand shook. "Take it. My purse is in the trunk."

His mouth, visible through a cut in the mask, twisted into a sinister smile. It iced her blood.

He stepped closer. The canvas grocery bags were wrapped around her wrist. The weight of the baby formula pulled them down. She gripped the handles.

"Please." Her voice trembled. "Just take the car and go."

She threw the keys at him. He instinctively reacted by trying to catch them. In one quick flash, she swung the canvas bags. The combined force of the baby formula cans knocked the gun from his hand. It clattered against the pavement. She swung again, aiming for his head. He stumbled and fell back.

Tara spun on her heel, gripped the shopping cart, and took off. The loose wheel vibrated violently. The sacks she'd stupidly hung on to banged between the metal grate of the cart and her knees. She opened her mouth to scream.

Something tackled her. She released the cart, and it skittered across the parking lot. Maddy's wails turned frantic.

Tara hit the asphalt and pain exploded across her hip and shoulder. The attacker slid across her. The air fled her lungs and tears pricked her eyes as she struggled to breathe. Maddy's cries echoed across the lot.

Move!

She struggled to her feet, but he grabbed her ankle. His gloved hand gripped hard enough to bruise bone. She twisted and kicked out with the other foot. The defensive move was meant for his nose but caught him on the shoulder instead. He yanked.

She scrambled to find purchase as the ground rushed

her. Her palms scraped against the asphalt and her head wacked against the side of a car's bumper. A red-hot flash of pain exploded across her vision.

The attacker loomed over her.

No! Maddy!

He grabbed her by the hair and slammed her head against the pavement.

Everything went black.

Grady joined the back of the checkout line and scanned the grocery store. Two people waited in front of him, and a lady and her five-year-old were in the next aisle over. No threats. Not that there would be many in Sweetgrass, Texas. A fact he'd reminded himself of over and over again. Still, years of working undercover had made him hyper-aware and extra vigilant. Becoming a Texas Ranger had intensified those habits.

He rubbed his palm against the ache in his bum leg. It hurt more today, probably due to all the driving. He'd spent the last two weeks working a murder case several counties over. At the end of the counter, the employee bagging groceries paused.

Tommy lifted a canvas sack. "Doctor Sims forgot her bag."

Tara? His heart skipped a beat. He hadn't seen her since Maddy's adoption proceeding.

"She must have been distracted by the baby's crying. I'll run it out to her," Tommy said to the cashier.

"And leave me without someone to bag my groceries?" The woman in line frowned. "She'll come back in and get it when she sees it's missing."

Grady stepped out of line and placed his items on the next register. "I'll take it to her, Tommy."

He grabbed the bag, his long strides eating up the distance between the register and the sliding doors. The moment they opened, Grady tensed.

The baby's scream carried on the wind. It was frantic. There was no way Tara would leave Maddy crying like that. He lowered the bag, silently dropping it on the sidewalk. His heart pounded as he ran toward the sound in a crouched position. A shopping cart sat against an unfamiliar vehicle at an odd angle. The baby's hands and feet waved from the carrier still resting on top.

Tara was nowhere in sight.

His heart broke for the baby and he wanted to comfort her, but first he had to find her mom. He pulled his gun and kept moving, keeping to the shadows. Canvas bags were spread around, a dented can of formula under a car's wheel. A few vehicles down, Tara came into view, lying on the ground. A man in a ski mask crouched over her.

"Police!" He pointed his gun at the attacker. "Freeze!"

The man raised his head. Their eyes met across the distance. It was too far to see clearly, but Grady sensed the attacker was weighing his options. Tara didn't move. He didn't know if she was breathing, and it killed him.

The attacker bolted. He scurried between two cars and grabbed something from an open trunk.

"Freeze!" Grady ordered. He could shoot him, but there was no way to know if anyone else was in the parking lot. He didn't want to run the risk of accidentally hitting an innocent bystander. The man disappeared into the shadows, his footsteps fading fast.

Grady's instincts were to take off after the attacker, but he couldn't leave Tara and the baby. He dropped to his knees next to her prone form. Holding his breath, he checked for a pulse on her delicate wrist.

She had a heartbeat. "Thank you, Lord."

There was so much blood on her face. He pulled out his phone. He rattled off his identification, requested an ambulance and additional units. He also gave them a description of the attacker—what little there was—and the direction he'd fled. They had to get him off the streets. If he was willing to attack a woman and child, who knew what else he would do?

Voices filtered across the parking lot. Tommy came around the corner. He was pushing a cart, the woman from earlier by his side. They spotted Grady and Tara at the same time and both stopped in their tracks, mouths dropping open.

"Tommy, check the baby."

The young man raced to the shopping cart.

"Is she hurt?" Grady barked out.

"She looks okay." He steered the entire cart over. Grady got up from his crouch, his leg screaming in protest. Maddy's wails had quieted. Her face was red from her efforts, and she'd shoved a tiny fist in her mouth. As Tommy had said, she appeared unharmed.

"Go inside and get me your first aid kit."

Sweetgrass was a small town with limited resources and the grocery store was on the outskirts. The police or ambulance might take fifteen minutes to get there. He needed to tend to Tara now.

The diaper bag was still inside the cart. He pulled out a burp cloth, and bent down to examine Tara. Other than the wound on her face, she seemed unharmed. Of course, it was impossible to know for sure until she was conscious or checked out by a doctor.

So much blood. Where was it coming from? Careful not to jostle her, he brushed his fingers along her skull. There was a wound hidden in her hair. He pressed the cloth to the gash.

Her eyes fluttered but didn't open.

"Tara, can you hear me?"

She didn't move and his tension racketed up. Head wounds could be deadly. The baby whimpered in her carrier.

"Stay with me, Tara. Maddy needs you. She can't lose you too."

TWO

Tara signed the discharge paperwork, scooped up her jacket, and winced. Her scraped palms stung, and her body ached with already sore muscles. Yet, she thanked God the injuries were minor. Things could have been so much worse.

In the parking lot, she'd regained consciousness with Grady hovering over her. The first thing he'd done was reassure her that Maddy was okay. The ER doctor had also thoroughly checked the baby over. Only then had Tara allowed treatment of her own injuries.

She bolted toward the waiting room. Although she knew Maddy was safe with Grady, she longed to hold her in her arms. She breathed a sigh of relief when they came into view through the glass doors.

Grady was leaning against the wall. His light brown hair was hidden underneath his white cowboy hat, and a five o'clock shadow darkened his square jaw. Blood—

hers?—stained the sleeve of his sports jacket. In his arms, he cradled a sleeping Maddy.

He closed the distance between them. "Are you okay?"

"Fine. A few stitches but that's all."

She held out her hands, and he carefully shifted Maddy to her arms. Tara cuddled her close and kissed the riot of curls at the top of her head. To think of what could have happened....

"Grady, I don't know how to thank you. I can't—"

A lump formed in Tara's throat and hot tears burned the back of her eyelids. She hadn't cried once. Not in the ambulance, not in the ER, not even when she'd given her statement to the detective. But now, with Maddy in her arms and the danger behind her, the emotions were overwhelming.

His warm hand grasped her upper arm and squeezed it gently. "There's no need to thank me. God put me in the right place at the right time. I'm glad you and Maddy weren't seriously hurt."

"Me too."

"Come on." Grady picked up the diaper bag and the carrier from a nearby chair. "Let's get the two of you home."

"That sounds like a good idea." She paused. "Wait, how are we going to get home? You rode in the ambulance with me."

"A couple of officers were nice enough to drop off my truck."

He hustled them outside. The temperature had

dropped and Tara's hands were icy by the time they got Maddy's car seat situated. She climbed into the cab. "I'm exhausted."

"It's normal after the night you've had." He pulled out of the hospital parking lot. "Seriously, are you okay? Any pain? I was worried you would have a concussion."

She was lucky she didn't after taking two knocks to the head. One when she hit the car's bumper and another when the attacker slammed her head against the ground.

"I'm okay." Ice had helped, as had the numbing medication, but she knew aspirin was in her future. "It's a good thing I'm hard-headed. It would've been difficult to spend the night in the hospital. I hate them."

His mouth twitched. "You're a doctor."

"Who doesn't work in a hospital. Besides, it's entirely different to be a patient."

"Ain't that the truth."

The street lights played with the edges of his strong profile. Her stomach fluttered. No matter how much she wished otherwise, he had an effect on her she couldn't shake. She'd never once thought of him romantically—not even when they were teenagers. But since her move back to town last year, whenever Grady walked into a room, her heart beat a touch faster. It was new and unfamiliar and horrifyingly similar to attraction. She didn't know what to do with it except pretend it wasn't happening.

"Do you want me to call Janet?" he asked. "I could have her meet us at your house."

Her best friend, Janet, was also Grady's younger sister.

"No, it's late. There's no need to bother her."

Silence descended. Despite the late hour, Grady's attention was laser sharp. His hands were firmly on the steering wheel and he kept checking the mirrors.

Tara fiddled with the cross around her neck. "When did you get back into town?"

"Tonight. The case was a rough one. Sorry about running out of the adoption proceeding straight after. I didn't have a lot of time to spare."

"I wasn't expecting you to come at all. It meant a lot you did."

Grady was part of her support system, which also included his parents and sisters. The West family had been a part of her life for as long as she could remember. Yet another reason why she refused to indulge in this fleeting attraction. To have the relationship go down in flames wouldn't just threaten her friendship with Grady, it would put the only family she had left at risk.

"It looked like everything went off without a hitch."

"It did. Vikki naming me as Maddy's guardian made the process straightforward. I wish her murder investigation was going as quickly."

Maddy's mother had been shot in cold blood on a deserted stretch of country road five months ago. Tara hated to think of Vikki's last moments, and now that she'd faced down a gunman herself, her imagination filled in the blanks far too well. Goose bumps broke out along her arms, and she hugged herself.

"I've been staying in touch with the detectives," Grady said. "They're running down every lead."

"I know." She sighed. "Do you think I should increase the reward? I can't believe no one saw her in the hours before her death."

She couldn't afford the money. Opening her own medical practice had taken most of her savings and the adoption had been an unexpected expense. But what could she do? Vikki didn't deserve to die that way, and Maddy, when she got older, would need answers.

"Hold on. Let me talk with the detectives more. Maybe I'll see some thread they haven't considered pulling yet." He glanced in the rearview mirror at Maddy in the car seat. "I'm just afraid the answers may not give her—or you—any comfort."

She wanted to disagree, but couldn't. Vikki, by her own admission, had a troubled past. Becoming pregnant with Maddy had been a catalyst for the single mother to turn her life around, but Tara was wise enough to know Vikki's past could have something to do with her murder. It was a heartbreaking proposition.

She bit her lip. "I never understood those parents who call in the middle of the night because their child has the hiccups. I mean, I got it, but I never *really* got it. Now, I do. Parenthood changes you. It's a messy ball of amazingness wrapped up in fear and paranoia. I want to smother her in cotton balls and keep her safe all the time, but logically, I know I can't. It's...I don't know. It's hard to describe."

"From what I can tell, it's normal. Happened to my sister. Lauren was the calmest of us all until the twins were born. Then she turned into a walking encyclopedia of warnings and dangers." He glanced at her. "It just means you care."

She did care. So much it was terrifying.

"I don't know when it happened, Grady. Sometime between Vikki's death and the adoption, I fell in love with her."

And she would do anything to keep Maddy safe. Anything.

Grady snuck a glance at Tara out of the corner of his eye. Her head rested against the back of the seat and her eyes were shut. Silky strands of hair played with the delicate curve of her cheek marred with a faint bruise. Ten to one, she was hurting and too stubborn to admit it. His jaw tightened. Whoever had attacked her was going to get his due.

Grady would make sure of it.

He pulled into her neighborhood. Tara's house was a small two-bedroom clapboard with blue shutters and a porch swing. Parking in the driveway, he scanned the area.

Quiet.

Tara opened her eyes, winced, and lifted a hand to her hair.

Grady frowned. "I'm calling Janet to come and stay the night."

"Please don't."

She placed a hand on his arm, stopping him. He

swore the heat of her touch went straight through the sleeve of his sports jacket.

"I need some pain medication and rest. That's all."

He hesitated, but it was the second time she'd said no. He wouldn't dismiss her wishes. Grady turned off the engine. "Let's get you guys inside."

He rounded the truck to open her door. She removed Maddy's car seat. The baby was still sleeping.

"I'll take her." His fingers brushed against Tara's as he grabbed the handle of the carrier. His heart skipped a beat. "You have your house keys?"

"Yes. The deputy found them in the parking lot." She frowned. "My car is still there. I need it to get to work tomorrow morning. And my groceries. I didn't even think about them."

"I have your groceries. They're in my truck, although not everything survived. Is Mom watching Maddy for you tomorrow?"

"Yes. She's been amazing. I couldn't open the clinic on Saturdays without her help, and it's made a huge difference for my patients with nine-to-five jobs."

"I'll pick you up in the morning and take you to your car. Then I'll drive Maddy out to the ranch." His boots thumped against the entry tile. "That way, you can sleep in a little longer. Problem solved."

He set the baby carrier on the dining room table. Tara's gaze bounced around, and she hurried to flip on several lights before unstrapping Maddy. The baby didn't stir.

"I'll do a quick check of your doors and windows before I leave. Make sure everything is secure."

"Thank you, Grady." She bit her lip. "It's probably silly to be worried—"

"Not at all. You've had a serious scare. I'll start in Maddy's room. That way you can lay her down and I won't accidentally wake her up."

He knew firsthand the dangers of waking a sleeping baby. Being shot had left him recuperating with a ridiculous amount of time on his hands. His older sister Lauren had twins around the same time. Helping to take care of his niece and nephew had saved his sanity and given him purpose during a period of his life he'd desperately needed it.

In the nursery, Grady checked the windows. All locked up tight. He moved on to the other rooms, methodically inspecting every entry point. When he circled back to the front door, he opened it.

He scanned the street, noting everything. The wind chimes on the porch, the beat-up truck two doors down, Vikki Spencer's empty house across the street. It smelled of damp grass and leaves. Somewhere a dog barked.

He went down the drive and opened his truck to retrieve Tara's groceries. Flashes of what might've transpired had he not interrupted the attack made his stomach churn. While waiting for Tara at the hospital, he'd alternated between worrying for her and running through the events in his mind. Something about the robbery was bothering him, but he couldn't quite pinpoint what it was.

He set the canvas bags on the dining room table. A flare of headlights made their way down the street. The vehicle slowed. Grady parted the curtains near the front door with the edge of his finger. The street light reflected off a Sweetgrass Police Department logo. He relaxed. The cavalry were here.

Footsteps came down the stairs. "What are you looking at?"

"Patrol car. I asked for special rounds around your house tonight." He dropped the curtain back into place. "It's nothing to be worried about. Just an extra precaution."

Her shoulders dropped. "You thought of everything."

"Believe it or not, it's my job." He tapped on the ranger badge pinned above his shirt pocket. "If you were to ask me to read an X-ray or prescribe antibiotics, I'm at a complete loss."

Her lips turned up at the corners. His breath hitched. Gosh, she was beautiful. It hit him every time he looked at her. She used to be his younger sister's pesky friend. Now, he saw her as anything but. Her hair was cut short, framing mahogany eyes and a face that was leaner and more defined than he remembered. But it was her personality that truly held him captive. Smart, honest, and unrelentingly kind.

He'd debated coming clean about his feelings, but held back. Getting involved with his sister's best friend was a hazardous proposition. Plus, Tara had an I'm-not-interested-so-don't-ask wall he couldn't quite figure out how to bypass.

"I'm going to make a cup of tea," she said. "Would you like some? I can scrounge up some of those buttery cookies you like so much."

"Well, if there's a cookie involved, I'm there."

She laughed. "Green tea, okay?"

He wouldn't know green tea from any other kind. He was a coffee man. But Tara obviously didn't want him to leave yet and he wasn't going anywhere until she was ready. "Whatever you have is fine."

He leaned against the divider between the kitchen and rest of the living area. Tara pulled out a container of cookies from the pantry and removed the lid. The scents of butter and vanilla wafted out. A warm feeling lodged in his chest to see the square ones with the sugar sprinkles—his favorite —hadn't been touched. Had she saved them for him?

Don't be ridiculous. He gave himself a mental shake. *They're Janet's favorite too.*

"Some night, huh?" Tara filled an electric kettle with water. "I bet you didn't think a quick run to the grocery store would end with saving a damsel in distress."

He snorted, fishing a cookie out of the pile. "You're no damsel in distress. The detective told me you knocked the gun out of the perpetrator's hands."

Her cheeks turned pink as she pulled two mugs down from the cabinet. "With the grocery sacks. Thank goodness the formula cans were heavy."

"Well, the weapon was recovered from the scene. Hopefully, we'll get forensics from it."

"The detective who took my statement said it was a

solid lead. Apparently, they've had several similar robberies in Navasota. He's hoping the gun will help them get this guy."

His phone beeped. He tossed the last bit of cookie in his mouth and read the text.

"They found your purse." The dessert turned sour in his stomach. The lingering sense of unease he'd been fighting with since the parking lot grew. "The money and credit cards were gone, along with your cell phone, but the rest of it appears to be intact. You won't have to replace your driver's license after all."

"Well, that's one small favor." She blew on her tea then took a sip. "I called the bank from the hospital and they hadn't had any fraudulent charges yet. All of that for the twenty dollars in cash in my wallet and my dry-cleaning slips."

Tara's shoulders were tense and her mouth tight. Continuing to talk about the attack wasn't going to help her sleep tonight. Time to change the subject.

"Tell me the truth. How stupid is the tux for my sister's wedding?" He arched his brows. "Are we talking bow tie and suspenders or just that silly thing that wraps around your waist?"

Her mouth quirked up. "You're in luck. No tux, just a suit. Plus, you get to keep your cowboy boots. At least, that's what I heard last. Now, if your mother gets involved, all bets are off."

He groaned. "I don't stand a chance against both Janet and my mother."

They joked and told stories. Twenty minutes later when Tara yawned, he set his mug down.

"Let me get out of here so you can get some rest."

She followed him to the door. "Thank you, Grady. For everything."

"No need to thank me." He paused on the stoop, resisting the urge to touch her one last time. "That's what friends do for each other. I'll see you in the morning. Don't forget to arm your security system."

"I won't."

The door closed behind him. He waited on the front porch until the snick of the lock slid into place, then went back to his truck and started the engine. He pulled out of the driveway and, slowly, circled the block.

Everything was quiet. Chances were, the loser in the parking lot was looking for a quick buck and had attacked Tara for her jewelry. Chasing down rabbit holes and improbable theories didn't often make sense, yet the incident left a bad taste in Grady's mouth.

Something about this wasn't right.

He pulled his phone from his pocket and dialed. "Hey, Luke, sorry to call so late, but I have a favor to ask."

THREE

The blade shimmered in the faint moonlight. He tightened his hand around the hilt. Across the street, Tara pulled Maddy from the back of a pickup truck. The baby was nothing more than a tiny lump encased in a blanket.

So close. He'd been so close.

He'd planned everything for weeks. A carefully orchestrated attack that would solve all of his problems in one fell swoop. His gaze jumped to Tara and his teeth ground together. She messed up everything. Everything!

He pressed the tip of the blade against the skin of his upper forearm. Blood beaded as he slowly, ever so slowly, sliced. Sharp pain radiated from the cut and warmth trickled down. In his mind, it was her skin he was slashing. Her blood flowing out.

Release. He unclenched his fist and took a deep breath. The pain brought clarity and kept the anger at bay. He couldn't lose control now. That was when mistakes were made, and things were already bad enough.

Grady West was a problem.

He didn't know the Texas Ranger personally, but he'd done enough research to have gathered two facts: his family was close to Tara and Grady wasn't someone to be underestimated.

Lights came on and, beyond the windows, shapes moved from room to room. The ranger was making sure the house was secure. He scoffed. As if he would be stupid enough to do anything tonight. He needed time to think. To plan. His gaze flickered to Maddy's room. The nightlight gave off the slightest glow.

Tara appeared in the upstairs window. She parted the curtains and stared down on the street. The light caressed her face, made her hair shimmer. His teeth ground together. How could she have fought him? He sliced with his blade. His arm throbbed and a fresh wave of warmth flowed down his skin. He closed his eyes, relishing the pain his knife wrought. She would be punished for her actions. He would make sure of that.

The door to the house opened and Grady came out. He stood on the porch scanning the street.

Keep looking. You can't see me, but I can see you.

He was smarter than all of them. If the ranger became a problem, he would take care of him too. No one was going to stand in his way.

Plan A hadn't worked. Never mind.

It was time to move to Plan B.

FOUR

Grady parked his truck on the far side of Burk's Grocers. The lot was empty save for one other state police vehicle and Tara's car. He settled his cowboy hat on his head, shading his eyes from the morning sunshine before grabbing the coffees he'd picked up on the way. There was a bit of a nip in the air, although the forecast called for loads of sunshine. His fellow ranger, Luke Tatum, was leaning against his truck but straightened when he spotted Grady.

Grady handed him a coffee. "Thanks for making the drive down."

"Not a problem." Luke flashed a grin. "I'm always glad to rack up another IOU. You never know when they will come in handy."

"Right now you're down by two, so don't get ahead of yourself."

It was all bluster. Rangers were part of a unique and

elite brotherhood. They always helped each other out. Company A was especially tight.

"I've already spoken to Chief Rodriguez," Luke said. "He's agreed, due to the special circumstances, to allow me to take the lead on this investigation."

Texas Rangers had jurisdiction over the entire state, but they only took the lead on cases after an invitation by local police and sheriffs' departments or, in rare cases, when it was mandated. Additionally, each ranger had an assigned geographical area. Grady lived in Sweetgrass but worked in nearby Huntsville and took care of the counties farther north. Tara's attack—along with the other robberies—had occurred in Grimes County, which was Luke's area.

"I'm not surprised he agreed so quickly. They don't get much crime like this here."

"I know. Navasota doesn't either." Luke took a long sip of his coffee. "How's your friend?"

"Shaken, but she's holding it together."

Luke started across the parking lot. "This her car?"

"Yes."

Grady gave him a rundown of the events, showing him where the baby had been in the cart, as well as where Tara was lying when he found her. In the daylight, it was easier to see details. Blood stained the asphalt. Her blood. The image of the attacker standing over her ate at him. If he'd been seconds later...

"What kind of jewelry was Tara wearing?"

Grady forced his attention away from the blood. "A diamond cross around her neck. The detective who took her initial statement believes that's why the robber attacked her."

Which only brought another wave of anger. The necklace had originally belonged to Tara's mother who'd died of brain cancer. She would've been devastated to lose it.

"You mentioned something about the scene was bugging you. Any ideas what?"

"Some." Grady ran a hand over his face. "The robbery almost felt like an afterthought. The perpetrator stole her purse as he was running away. He doesn't attempt to use her credit cards. He doesn't steal her ID. It left me with questions."

"You're afraid this is personal?"

"I'd like to rule it out."

"Well, the case sounds similar to the ones in Navasota," Luke said. "The perpetrator wears black clothing, including a ski mask, and always uses a gun. He targets women, snatching their purses and sometimes their jewelry. The previous robberies have all taken place in parking lots. A grocery store, like this one, a strip mall, and a pharmacy."

Grady heard a tone in Luke's voice. "But?"

"Not once did he ever bother to take out the light."

Glass crunched under the heel of Grady's boot as he moved closer to Tara's car. The sedan was sprinkled with the remnant shards of the light she'd parked underneath. His mouth flattened. "That's not easy to do."

"No. It's difficult to hit the right angle and have enough force."

"He took out the light for additional protection. Maybe because Tara can identify him?"

Was that the aspect tugging at Grady? Had he subliminally recognized the way the perpetrator moved?

"Possibly. If he was simply after her purse and car, the dark clothes and ski mask would have been enough. There are some additional inconsistencies between this crime and the others. All the other women described the perpetrator as being around five-eight and two hundred fifty pounds."

"That's not this guy. He's over six foot and roughly two hundred pounds."

"There's one more thing. The third woman he attempted to rob fought back."

"Was she hurt?"

Luke shook his head. "The attacker ran away. It doesn't necessarily mean this isn't connected, but coupled with the difference in physical descriptions I'm inclined to think this isn't the same guy. Could be we have two men working together to rob women. Or it's possible your instincts are spot-on and this is a personal attack made to look like something else."

Grady's gaze shot to the bloodstain on the asphalt. His stomach tightened. "How much of the information you gave me was in the papers?"

"All of it." Luke's tone was grim. "Is there any reason why someone would attack Tara?"

"Not that I know of." Grady shoved his hands in his pockets. "However, she recently adopted a baby from a neighbor who was murdered five months ago. The case hasn't been solved yet."

"You're wondering if the two incidents are connected?"

"I find the timing curious. Tara has set up a reward for information that leads to an arrest, plus she's been pushing the detectives for answers. Vikki Spencer was shot four times while parked on Old Greer Road. It was done in the middle of the night and there are no witnesses. Her purse and cell phone were left in the vehicle, untouched. It's like the guy drove up, shot her, and fled. Now Tara is attacked by a masked gunman in a parking lot. Coupled with the differences between this crime and the other robberies, it only makes me more suspicious. Maybe someone wants us to believe these are two separate cases, but they aren't."

"That's a stretch, Grady."

It was. But getting shot had taught Grady never to ignore an investigation thread unless the evidence showed him otherwise. "But not impossible."

"No." Luke was quiet for a moment. "Listen, chances are this is connected to the robberies in Navasota, but I'm not one to take options off the table. I'll put a rush on the gun recovered from the scene. Maybe we'll get prints or a hit on ballistics."

One of the benefits of having a case worked by a Texas Ranger was getting priority at the state lab.

"Since you've been in contact with the detectives investigating Vikki's murder, can you clear the way for me to look at the file?" Luke asked. "Never hurts to make sure nothing was missed. Besides, if someone is trying to silence Tara to prevent Vikki's case from being solved, the more people looking into it, the better."

The vise around Grady's chest loosened. Tara and Maddy were in good hands. Not just his, but Luke's too.

"Consider it done. And, Luke, I appreciate it."

His friend grinned. "Enough to consider us even in IOUs?"

Grady laughed. "Don't push it."

"So, it's not Ebola?"

Tara shifted Maddy in her arms, struggling to keep the phone between her shoulder and ear while she opened the garage door. Tuesdays were supposed to be her day off—a trade, since she worked on Saturdays—but who was she kidding? This was the fourth call from a patient today. She dropped her keys.

"No, it's definitely not Ebola." The garage door gave a squeal and opened. "In fact, Mr. Williamson, you are healthier than men half your age. As I said in the office yesterday, I suspect it's a mild virus. Plenty of fluids and rest should do the trick."

"Are you sure?"

"Mr. Williamson, we've discussed this before. Using an internet web service to look up your symptoms can be helpful, but it will also give you a broad range of diagnoses, including the worst-case scenarios."

Tara loaded Maddy into her car seat while her

patient muttered something about no-good doctors before he hung up. She chuckled. Mr. Williamson was cranky and irritable, but he was also lonely. Half of his visits were to have someone to talk to. Ten to one, he was going to be back in her office tomorrow, convinced he had the bubonic plague. No, that was last week. Maybe—

A shadow loomed. She gasped and spun, nearly tripping over her feet in the process. Her phone dropped from her shoulder. A hand shot out and caught it.

"Hey, hey, hey. Are you okay?"

She blinked as her brain caught up with her eyes. She sucked in a breath. "Ken. You startled me."

"I'm sorry. I called your name, but I guess you didn't hear me." Her neighbor opened his palm, revealing her phone. "Thank goodness this didn't hit the cement."

She plucked it from his hand. "Especially since it's new. Good catch. Thank you."

"Sure thing."

Maddy fussed. Ken reached into the car and pulled on the string of the toy hanging from the car seat. Pop Goes the Weasel played. He laughed and adjusted his wire-rim glasses. "That has got to drive you insane. I didn't try it at the store before I bought it. Guess I should have."

"Not at all. It makes her happy." She opened the driver's side door and tossed her purse inside. "I haven't seen you around lately. We missed you at church on Sunday."

"I was working. We're short-staffed at the moment, so I've been picking up some double shifts."

Ken worked as a tech specialist for a security company in the next town. Dark circles hung under his eyes and his skin was pale. He was working himself too hard.

On the street, a patrol car rolled past. Tara raised her hand in a wave and the officer gestured back.

"They've been making a lot of rounds on the street the last couple of days," Ken said, jerking his thumb at the patrol car. "Any idea what's going on?"

"I was robbed on Saturday night in the grocery store parking lot."

His eyes widened behind the rims of his glasses. "Are you...well, obviously you're all right. What happened?"

"It's still under investigation. The short story is my purse was stolen. The guy got away but the police are working hard on the case."

It was the same story she told everyone. The bare facts and nothing else. Truth was, she didn't have much more than that. It terrified her to think about the attack in the parking lot and the way the man had threatened her. Thank goodness for Grady. Not only had he stuck close, but he'd arranged for Sweetgrass PD to keep watch as well.

"That's horrible." Ken shook his head. "I'm glad you weren't hurt."

"Thanks. Me too." She paused. "Did you need to talk about something in particular or were you just dropping in to say hi?"

"Oh, I hate to bother you. Never—"

"No, no. Please," she encouraged.

Ken was always considerate. It was one of the things that made him such a great neighbor. She hated to think he needed something but didn't want to ask because he'd learned of the attack.

"What's going on?"

He reached into the back pocket of his slacks and pulled out a sheet of paper. His nails had been bitten down nearly to the quick. "Ma's numbers are terrible. She's not taking her medicine like she should and she's eating sweets, even though I've explained to her a hundred times it's not good for her diabetes."

Tara scanned the numbers. "I can see why you're concerned. These are much higher than they should be."

"Is there any way you can talk to her? Convince her to take better care of herself?" His mouth pursed. "With Wayne back in the house, it's creating an impossible situation. He doesn't take her diagnosis seriously."

Tara's heart went out to him. He didn't get along with his older brother. Wayne's criminal streak had created a host of trouble for his family. She folded the paper and handed it back. "Bring your mom in. I won't make any promises but hopefully, between the two of us, we'll convince her to take her diabetes more seriously."

"She lives far and I work most days. I won't be off in time to make it during office hours."

"No problem. Just call the office and let Carol know what day you can do it. I'll stay late."

His shoulders dropped. "Thanks, Tara. You have no idea how much this has been weighing on me."

"Of course. It's not a problem."

She crossed the garage and picked up her keys from the floor where they'd fallen before jiggling the back door knob to make sure it was locked.

"There's one more thing," Ken said. "I was cleaning my roof last week and noticed a hole in Vikki's eave. I've seen some squirrels around and I'm worried they've gone inside and made a nest in her attic."

Tara's gaze went to the empty house across the street. It was next door to Ken's, and together they'd been working to keep an eye on it. While Vikki had made arrangements for Maddy's guardianship, she hadn't done anything regarding her assets. Tara hadn't been given the legal authority to sell the house yet.

"Animals in the attic could create a huge mess." She checked her watch. Mr. Williamson's phone call had delayed her. So had the conversation with Ken. She had errands to run before meeting with Janet to try on wedding dresses. "I can't check it now, but I promise to do it later on tonight. Thanks for letting me know."

FIVE

"This wedding dress makes me look like a peacock." Janet blew an errant curl off her face and eyed herself in the full-length mirror. "What was my aunt thinking?"

Tara cleared her throat to hide the laugh bubbling up. "The feathers are a bit much."

"A bit? Let's be honest. Maddy and I could go to the Halloween fair tonight as zoo animals."

Maddy blew raspberries and smacked at the toy attached to her stroller. The clear ball spun, rattling the smaller, more colorful shapes within. Hanging from the stroller was the baby's costume for the fair later tonight. She was going to be a lion, complete with the cutest mane and ears.

"Watch," Janet continued. "Two out of my five crazy relatives will love it and World War Fifteen will commence."

She lifted her skirt, revealing ballerina flats and

marched out. A chorus of ahhs was canceled out by an emphatic no.

"I don't know what you're talking about, Mama." Janet's voice filtered into the dressing room. "It's gorgeous. I feel positively royal."

Tara clapped a hand over her mouth, her stomach clenching with laughter. Moments later, her best friend strolled back in. Her lips were pressed together—probably to keep from giggling—and her eyes twinkled.

"You're terrible." Tara shook her head. "Absolutely terrible."

"If they're going to make me try on the most hideous dresses in the shop, I may as well have fun." Janet turned her back so Tara could undo the zipper. "Besides, while they're fighting we can talk. Has there been any news about the attack?"

"Not yet. By the way, thanks again for coming over the other night. I didn't realize a double feature and brownie sundaes were what I needed, but it felt so good to laugh."

"There's nothing that can't be fixed by chocolate and a great comedy. We should do it more often. In fact, we could even go out next week. Todd's been wanting to see the latest action flick and now that Grady's back in town, we could all see it together."

She shot her friend a look. "Don't start matchmaking."

"I'm not." Janet's mouth twitched. "Okay, maybe I am a little. But you guys have been spending a lot of time together lately. I mean, you're going to the

Halloween festival together. You can't stop a girl from trying."

Tara handed the gown to the clerk waiting outside the dressing room and shook her head. "Your brother and I are just friends. He's been sticking close because of the attack, which I appreciate, but it's as simple as that."

Janet pressed her lips together. Whatever she wanted to say, it was killing her to keep it in.

"What is it?"

"I'm not trying to rock the boat, Tara, but I've seen the way you look at him sometimes. There's a spark there, and it's been obvious ever since you moved back to town."

She wanted the carpet to open and swallow her whole. If Janet had noticed the shift in her feelings, who else had? Had Grady? Heat rose in her cheeks.

Janet's eyes twinkled. "It's obvious to *me* because I've known you since the first grade."

"Stop doing that."

"Reading your mind? But I'm so good at it."

"I—"

A quick rap cut the conversation off. Janet's mother popped her head into the dressing room. "Since you two gabby gusses are taking forever, Tara, can I borrow Maddy? It might be nice if the flower girl had a tiara."

"Sure thing."

Maddy caught sight of Deeann and bounced in the stroller. Janet's mother was one of her favorite people. The baby flashed her an open-mouthed grin.

Deeann laughed. "She is such a cutie."

She efficiently maneuvered the stroller out of the

dressing room. "And you two get moving. The store is closing soon because of the Halloween festival, and we'll never get done at this rate. The wedding is in a month. It's a wonder I don't have a full head of gray hair from all the stress."

The velvet curtains dropped down behind her. Janet shook her head. "You know she's going to pick the biggest tiara possible."

"No sense in fighting it. She'll get her way anyway. It's a Jedi mind trick Southern mothers have perfected." Tara selected the next gown from the rack and draped it open. "You heard her. Less talking, more dresses."

"Hold on," Janet stepped into the gown and shoved her arms in the sleeves, "we didn't finish our original conversation. So, you're telling me there is no chance you would date Grady?"

Would Grady even want to date her? There was attraction on her side, but she had been so careful to avoid applying anything more to his actions than simple friendship. She was tempted to ask but tamped down the impulse. It didn't matter what Grady thought.

"I like our relationship the way it is."

Anything else would just be too complicated. Boyfriends had always been a take-it-or-leave-it thing for her. But Grady...she sensed he wasn't like the other men she'd dated. He would dig in deep to her heart and she refused to give anyone the power to hurt her like her father had done to her mother.

Tara circled around and, without stepping on the train, scooted herself close enough to the gown to close the back. "Besides, you don't want me dating your brother. I'm terrible at romance."

"Maybe you just haven't tried with the right person."

She snorted. "That's only what people madly in love say."

Janet placed her hands on her cheeks. "Oh no. I've become one of those women, haven't I? The ones who gush about their fiancés and constantly set single people up. I always hated them, and now I'm a member of the club."

"You're forgiven. Love looks good on you." She stepped back to take in the gown and her mouth twitched. "That dress however...not so much."

Janet looked in the mirror. "Ack! This one is worse than the last and that's saying something. Maybe I should elope."

"Don't even think about it. Your parents would have a conniption fit. Besides, the wedding is in a few weeks. It's not like you have much longer to go anyway."

"Thank goodness." She hiked up the dress and walked toward the door. "Hey, Tara. In all seriousness, don't let our relationship hold you back if you have feelings for Grady. We're all adults. We can handle it."

The words seemed to hang in the air after Janet left. They taunted her resolve to keep Grady squarely in the friend zone. Seeing her friend so happy and in love also made Tara question her own decision to remain single.

Until she thought of her father.

He'd walked out when she was five, traded them up for a younger wife, and started a new family three states over. Her mother had been devastated and Tara had learned a hard-won lesson. Happily ever after didn't always happen.

No, it was better to keep her distance and play it safe. Especially when it came to Grady since—

A scream tore through the store. Several more followed and Tara's pulse kicked into high gear. She ran from the dressing room.

Janet's aunt lay dazed and bleeding on the floor. People rushed to her side. Others, including Janet and her mother, were moving toward the front of the store. Through the glass, a man in a clown costume ran down the sidewalk pushing a stroller.

Her stroller. With Maddy in it.

Tara sprinted across the carpet, and burst out of the store.

"Stop that man! He's kidnapped my baby!"

The lingering sunlight cast long shadows as Grady made his way to the bridal store. The Halloween festival was kicking off. Parents with children dressed in costumes crossed the parking lot toward Main Street, which had been closed off for the activities. The scents of pretzels and popcorn mingled with fresh cut grass. Several people called out a hello as he passed them.

It was his childhood all over again. That was the amazing thing about Sweetgrass. Time moved at a snail's pace and change, while inevitable, rarely shifted the landscape. After more than a decade working undercover, it was a relief to be home again. He'd stretched his roots, tested the limits, but they'd held strong.

He rounded the corner of the building. His sister stood on the sidewalk, dressed in a wedding gown. She was speaking rapidly to someone on the phone. Inside the bridal shop, a group of women surrounded someone on the floor.

Tara? He started running.

Janet spotted him. "Grady, thank goodness. A guy dressed as a clown kidnapped Maddy. Tara's chasing him. I'm on the phone with 911."

"Which way?"

She pointed and he sprinted off. How far had they gotten? Was he too late? Weaving through people he darted into the alley between two buildings. On the other side, people were looking and pointing. He caught sight of Tara's dark hair half a second before it disappeared.

He took off after her. A group of people emerged from a restaurant and blocked the sidewalk.

"Police," he shouted. "Move!"

A toddler jumped in his path. Grady swerved and narrowly missed him. Sharp pain stabbed his thigh. He took the corner of a building and scraped his arm on the brick wall. Tara came into view and so did a man in a clown costume.

Grady added another burst of speed and passed Tara. His boots pounded against the pavement. The man was headed for the parking lot on the far side of Main Street. He had to catch him before he jumped into a vehicle. If the kidnapper drove off with Maddy, it would be much harder to find them. He pushed his legs to their maximum.

Another few inches.

Grady reached out. His fingers brushed against the costume's fabric but slid off the silky material. The man glanced back and his eyes widened. He made a sharp turn. Grady tried to match it but his thigh, already pushed beyond anything he'd recuperated for, gave way. He stumbled.

The perpetrator darted down a small path into the park and disappeared. Grady took a shortcut through a set of flowerbeds, Tara right behind him. Branches tore at his clothes. One scratched his face. He burst through the trees and came up short. Families gathered at the bouncy houses. A mom wrangled a toddler dressed as Spider-man. Grady scanned for a clown but saw nothing.

Chest heaving, Tara cried, "Where is he?"

Grady bolted for the parents waiting at the face-painting area. "Texas Ranger. Did you see a clown pushing a stroller?"

One man pointed. "He went that way."

Grady ran. His cowboy hat flew off his head, landing somewhere in the park. He dashed past the playground, and a flash of red caught his attention. A clown wig. Willing more speed into his legs, he pushed forward. The kidnapper had made a fatal error. In his haste to get away from Grady, he'd diverted toward the games area on the far side of the festival. Officers stood directing traffic on the busy street. The kidnapper was heading straight for them. Grady opened his mouth—

"Stop that man!" Tara shouted behind him. "Kidnapper!"

The officers broke into a run. The kidnapper shoved the stroller. It bounced across the pavement, barely slowing. Viewers shouted from the Ferris wheel. The stroller, along with Maddy, flew into the street. A truck barreled toward the baby.

Grady surged forward. He launched himself, shoving the stroller with the sheer force of his body. Together they flew onto the opposite sidewalk. Grady hit the ground and rolled. The screeching of the truck's tires muffled the sound of Tara's screams.

SIX

Tara's pulse wouldn't settle into a normal rhythm. More than an hour later, the mental image of the truck heading straight for Grady and Maddy was enough to send ice water rushing through her veins. The very prospect that the kidnapper had gotten away was too horrible to contemplate.

She paced the length of the conference room in the Sweetgrass Police Department. Twelve steps. She turned and went back. Maddy wriggled and fussed. She was tired of being held, but Tara couldn't convince herself to put her down. She grabbed a rattle from the table and shook it.

The police station was nearly empty. Most of the officers were out at the fair searching for the kidnapper, along with Grady and several of his fellow rangers. But he hadn't left her to wait alone with Maddy. Grady's father stood guard next to the conference room doorway.

Raymond's hair was mostly gray now, the lines in his face deepened from a life of working outside on the land, but his shoulders were still broad and his posture ramrod straight. A former military sniper, he could shoot with dangerous precision. A skill Tara was hopeful he wouldn't have to use anytime soon.

"Maybe we should ask the officer at the front desk if they've learned anything new," she said. "It's been over an hour since the detective took my statement."

Raymond's eyes softened when he glanced at her. "It takes time to work an investigation like this. They have to question witnesses. Gather video. Grady will give us an update when he can. Until then, we just have to be patient."

Waiting. It gave her too much time to think.

"I've got coffee and sandwiches." Deeann bustled into the room. Her long skirt flowed around her legs as she drew to a stop and set several bags and a coffee tray on the table. She smiled at Tara. "I also brought your favorite soup, dear."

Tara couldn't eat or drink anything. Her stomach was in knots, but the gesture was kind and she didn't want to hurt Deeann's feelings. "It smells wonderful."

Tara's phone beeped with an incoming text, and she scooped it up from the table. "It's from Janet. Aunt Rosie is fine. No concussion or any other serious injury, but the doctor warned her to take it easy since she was knocked on the head."

"Thank goodness."

Deeann echoed Tara's own thoughts. They were lucky no one had gotten seriously hurt. This time. But how would she keep Maddy safe? The kidnapping had been in daylight with crowds of people around.

Through the glass, she saw Grady stroll into the police station. He was limping slightly and fighting against it. His hair was mussed and still bore a faint ring from his missing cowboy hat. A scrape edged his strong jaw. His lips were thinned into a hard line, his shoulders tense.

Deeann let out a small sigh. "Oh, no…"

Tara didn't need an interpretation. She could see it written in Grady's expression.

The kidnapper had gotten away.

He entered the room, his focus locked on Tara. "Sorry to keep you waiting. I wanted to be thorough."

"Do you have anything to go on?" Raymond asked.

Grady ran a hand through his hair. "Some witnesses but no one who could identify the kidnapper beyond the clown costume. Between the wig and the face paint, he could have been anyone. The kidnapper pushed the stroller away from him to create a distraction, and it worked. While everyone was focused on Maddy, he disappeared."

"Tara, honey, I think it would be a good idea for you and Maddy to stay with us tonight." Deeann placed a hand on her arm. "With Raymond and Grady on the ranch, there won't be a shortage of protection."

"More than tonight," Raymond echoed. "You'll stay with us until everything is sorted out."

"I don't want to put you in danger—"

"Nonsense," Grady cut her off. "The ranch is the best place for you and Maddy. Plus, you can leave Maddy with Mom and Dad when you need to see patients."

She had already planned on canceling most of her appointments tomorrow. But Grady was right. She couldn't disappear from her job. The closest hospital was forty miles away. For some of Sweetgrass's residents, it might as well be a hundred. Her own mother had died from brain cancer because it hadn't been detected early enough. Having a doctor in town saved lives, and she wouldn't put her patients at risk.

"It's settled then," Deeann said. "Raymond, let's take our coffee to the break room so Grady and Tara can talk."

The room emptied out, leaving Grady and Tara alone. She moved toward him. How could she begin to express the emotions inside her? He'd risked his life to save Maddy. The baby bounced in her arms and, the moment she was close enough, launched herself at Grady. Tara could hardly blame her. She wanted to throw herself into the lawman's strong arms too.

"Glad to see you still like me, darlin'." Grady patted the baby's back. "I was worried we wouldn't be friends anymore."

His attention shifted to Tara. "You're sure she's all right? She didn't get hurt?"

"She's fine, thanks to you. The stroller never even tilted over."

He held up two fingers about an inch apart. "I was

this close to catching him and putting an end to this whole thing."

"It's not your fault." She'd seen his leg give out while chasing the kidnapper. She couldn't stand the thought of him blaming himself. "You saved Maddy. That was the most important part. You're a hero in my eyes."

His gaze met hers. The coldness she'd been fighting with since the kidnapping melted away. Tara thought she'd never feel safe again, and yet here with Grady, she did.

He wouldn't let anything happen to her. Or Maddy.

She reached up to take his chin with her two fingers and gently turned his head. "That's a nasty scrape on your jaw."

"I'm fine."

He pulled away, and she dropped her hand. What was she doing? Grady was her friend. They didn't touch like this. She was crossing a line.

"I got your text. What is it, Tara?"

The kidnapping had inevitably made her think of the attack from earlier in the week and she'd had a few new realizations.

"The guy who assaulted me in the parking lot stared at Maddy. I didn't place any significance on it until today, but now...things are different." She bit her lip. "That's why he didn't steal my purse out of the trunk or take the car keys when I offered them. What he wanted wasn't money. He was after Maddy."

No shock filtered across his features. They stayed hard. Determined.

"You've already figured that out."

"I'm not taking anything off the table yet, but yes, I believe the two attacks are linked. And if Maddy was the target, it would explain why the robber stole your purse like it was an afterthought and why he chased after you when you ran."

A chill ran down her spine. "But why? Why kidnap Maddy?"

———

Maddy placed a dimpled hand on Grady's cheek and smiled, flashing two tiny teeth. His chest squeezed tight. If he'd been just seconds later...His gaze shifted to Tara. His own fears were reflected in her eyes. It killed him to see her hurting. A wave of anger followed, so fierce it was blinding.

"We are going to catch this guy, Tara. I promise you."

It wasn't in his nature to make promises. They were fragile things, especially for law enforcement where cases could sometimes take unexpected turns. This one, however, he had every intention of keeping.

But in order to do that, he had to keep his head in the game. He'd felt Tara's touch clear to his bones. Their friendship was shifting, the sands underneath them testing the glue of their foundation. He wanted to believe there was something more between them, but he also had to face reality. Tara was in emotional turmoil. Her child had almost been kidnapped right before her eyes. It wouldn't be wise to attribute anything she did now as a true indication of her feelings.

Luke came into the station. Grady opened the conference room door and waved him inside.

"West, you look good with a baby."

"I look good in every situation," he ribbed back. "Try not to be jealous."

Grady turned. "Luke, this is Tara Sims. Tara, this is Luke Tatum. All joking aside, there's no one better to have watching your back than him."

"Pleasure to meet you, ma'am, although I'm sorry for the circumstances." Luke shook her hand. "I want to assure you we have the very best on the case. Keeping you and the baby safe is our top priority."

"Thank you."

"Grady, can I talk to you for a moment?"

"No." Tara's gaze jumped back and forth between them. "Whatever information you have, I want to hear it. I can't keep Maddy safe from what I don't understand."

Luke sent Grady a questioning look and he nodded. Tara was Maddy's mother. She deserved to know what was going on.

"Let's all sit down." His leg was killing him, not that he would admit it if asked. "No sense in having this conversation standing up."

Maddy reached for Tara, and she pulled the baby into her lap. Grady took the chair next to them.

"The ballistics came back on the gun Tara knocked out of the perpetrator's hand," Luke said. "It's a match to the one that killed Vikki Spencer."

All of the blood drained from her face. "Whoever killed Vikki is now trying to kidnap Maddy?"

"It looks that way. Good call on your part, Grady. If we hadn't rushed it to the front of the line, it would've taken a lot longer to put the pieces together."

"You knew?" Tara's voice rose. "You knew and you didn't say anything."

"I didn't know until right this moment."

Dread gripped his throat. The kidnapper had tried twice to get his hands on Maddy. Both times had been in public places. That demonstrated determination. If the same person had also murdered Vikki Spencer, he was capable of anything.

"I knew Vikki had been murdered," he explained. "I suspected something wasn't right with the robbery. But I wasn't sure the two cases were linked. That's why I warned you to be careful and had Sweetgrass police tailing you for the last few days."

Her shoulders dropped and she rubbed her forehead. "Of course. I just…"

"I know." She hadn't been prepared and he was to blame. "I thought you were the target. I never suspected it was Maddy."

The baby banged on the table with a small hand.

"What made you think I was the target?"

"Because you were creating a fuss over Vikki's murder and pushing for answers. I was worried the killer had gotten wind of it and was trying to get rid of you." His jaw clenched. "I was wrong."

"The million-dollar question is, why would anyone

49

murder Vikki and then wait five months before attempting to kidnap Maddy?" Luke asked. "Tara, did Maddy get any inheritance when Vikki died?"

She shook her head. "Nothing. Vikki had a small life insurance policy, which covered the cost of her funeral. Her house is in probate, but most of it is owned by the bank."

"So, the motive isn't financial. Where's Maddy's father?"

"I don't know. Vikki never talked about him. All she would say is that he was in the military and deployed. Shortly before Maddy was born, she told me he died in Afghanistan. We were required to try and locate him as part of the adoption process, but weren't able to. I don't even know his name and nothing in any of Vikki's personal effects indicated things were different from what she said."

Grady frowned. "The adoption was finalized two weeks ago. What would happen if Maddy's father showed up now? Could he obtain custody?"

Her eyes widened. "His rights were terminated. He wouldn't have any claim on Maddy."

"Well, that might explain why she's being kidnapped," Luke said.

"But why wouldn't Maddy's father just come forward before everything was settled? He could've stopped the adoption."

Grady considered the question. "He'd committed murder. An unsolved murder. And while there wasn't much physical evidence to go on, there was always the chance law enforcement would put two and two together. Especially since you were pushing so hard to have Vikki's murder solved. Maybe he was scared. Maybe he was trying to figure out how to come forward without raising suspicion."

"And then time ran out," Tara whispered.

"Now the only way he can get Maddy is to take her. He sees the other robberies in the news and gets the idea to copycat them. He wants to make it look like a carjacking gone wrong. You're shot and Maddy disappears. What he didn't count on was you fighting back."

"Or you showing up to rescue me."

His gaze locked with hers. There was something there, buried in those mahogany depths, he hadn't seen before. His heart double-timed.

Luke cleared his throat. "Okay, so I'm open to ideas on how we find out the identity of Maddy's father."

"Vikki does have a brother," Tara offered. "Dan Spencer. I've asked him about Maddy's father before. Dan swears he doesn't know anything, but I've always sensed he was holding back."

"Why?"

"He wanted the adoption to go through. If he told me or the court about Maddy's father, it would've complicated things. Now she's in danger and the adoption is finalized. Dan might be more honest under these circumstances."

Grady stood. "I'll need his address."

"No, you won't." Her chin tilted up. "I'm coming with you."

"That's not a good idea."

"Actually, it's a very good idea. Dan has had some trouble with the law. Nothing big, but he's wary of cops. He won't talk to you. If I go, he will."

Luke smirked at Grady. "Sounds like you have a partner."

SEVEN

Dan Spencer lived near the county line. A crooked and bullet-ridden sign announced the subdivision: West Side Trailer Park. Tara slowed her vehicle and turned in.

"Remember, do exactly as I tell you."

"I already promised five times." She rolled her eyes. "Relax, Grady. Dan has had bumps in his life, but he's not a bad guy. I've been out here a couple of times."

If several arrests for B&Es and a history of drugs were her definition of a couple of bumps, they should have a talk. He shifted in his seat. He didn't like being the passenger, but he'd landed on his bad leg when rescuing Maddy and it was already swollen. Driving would aggravate it.

"He lives on the end. Number 35."

They passed a rusted-out Ford, several bicycles, and a couple of children without shoes playing tag. Dan's trailer was the last in the row. It was tidier than his neighbors. A small front porch, clean chrome, and a trash-free yard. A plant sat next to the welcome mat.

Grady recognized Dan. They'd never met, but he'd seen his latest arrest photo. Drugs. Dan had spent two years in prison for selling meth. It was immediately clear he'd changed for the better. His face was no longer gaunt and his build looked healthy. He wore a tan jumpsuit stitched with Harvey Yard Service across the right pocket.

Maybe Tara was right and he had turned his life around.

Dan lifted his hand in greeting to Tara and then squinted at the passenger side. She got out of the car, and Grady followed. His leg protested every step toward the porch.

"Hey, Dan." She pointed to the cigarette in his hand. "I thought you were going to stop."

"I tried. Didn't take." He rose to greet her with a smile. "Don't start getting all doctory on me. Who's your friend?"

"Grady West." He stepped forward and stretched out his hand.

Dan didn't move. "You're a cop."

"A Texas Ranger."

His brows snapped together. "What's going on? Where's Maddy?" Dan looked back toward the car. His voice rose. "You've never come without Maddy."

If Dan was acting he deserved an award. There was little doubt in Grady's mind, the man cared deeply about his niece.

Of course, the kidnapper's intentions likely weren't to hurt Maddy. He'd shoved the stroller, yes, but it had gone into the street by accident and the kidnapper's reaction had been out of panic when he realized Grady was getting too close. No, whoever was behind this probably loved—or thought he loved—the little girl.

"Maddy's fine," Tara said. "She's absolutely fine."

Dan let out a breath, but his shoulders didn't lose their tension. "Something bad's happened, huh? You wouldn't bring a cop here if something bad hadn't happened."

"We do need to talk."

She gently steered him to the lawn chair. Dan sat and the woven strings stretched under his weight.

"What is it?" He took a long drag of the cigarette before snuffing it out. Smoke blew from his nostrils.

Tara sat in the only other chair on the porch and Grady leaned against the railing. He was careful to put distance between himself and Dan, yet still be between the other man and Tara. He wanted to protect her, but he also had to be careful not to intrude. Dan would probably say more if he wasn't hyperaware of Grady's presence.

"Dan, I need to know who Maddy's father is."

He reared back in his chair. "Why? The adoption is finalized."

"Some things have happened recently, and it's become important. If you know who he is, you need to tell me."

Dan's gaze darted toward Grady. "What things?"

"Someone has attempted to kidnap Maddy twice."

The other man's mouth dropped open. "What?"

Dan's fingers twitched. Against his pants. It was slight and something most people would miss. But Grady wasn't most people. He'd worked undercover. His life had literally depended on being able to read people.

Dan had known about the kidnapping attempts.

"They haven't been successful," Grady interjected. "Your niece is fine."

Dan ignored him, keeping his attention on Tara. "What happened?"

She relayed the events of the last week in measured and even tones, sharing only the information he would be able to glean from news reports. They'd already agreed to not mention the attacks were linked to Vikki's murder. That fact would stay under wraps for as long as possible. The kidnapper was already desperate enough, no need to add fuel to the fire.

When she was done, Dan lit up a new cigarette. He took a long drag. "You think Maddy's dad has something to do with this?"

"It's the only reason I can think of for someone to take her."

He let out the smoke in a long stream. "I've told you before, I don't know who he is."

"But you do suspect someone," she pushed.

"I don't want to get him in trouble. Especially when I ain't sure if he's the guy. It's not right."

Grady's teeth ground together. Maddy had nearly been kidnapped. If there was ever a time to spill the beans, now was it. As a man, he wanted to rip the information from Dan's mouth. As a professional, he understood it was better to let Tara convince him.

"Dan, this is Maddy we're talking about." She perched on the edge of her chair. The back of it rose. "I understand your reluctance, but there's nothing more important than protecting her."

Dan took another two puffs. His leg jittered. "Okay. But remember, this is my own suspicion. Vikki never told me."

"I understand."

"I always thought Maddy's daddy was Travis Cobb."

Grady recognized the name. Travis was known for two things: getting into trouble and fixing cars. As a youth, his name had been said by law enforcement with the same stress as a curse word. Lately, if rumors were to be believed, Travis had cleaned up his act. He was married and owned a small automotive shop on the far side of town.

"Travis Cobb?" Tara frowned. "Why Travis?"

"Vikki had a thing for him in high school. She used to follow him around like a puppy dog." He crossed his leg over his knee. "Truth is, Vikki always had a thing for a bad boy. Even later. Anyway, around the time of...well, around the time she got pregnant with Maddy, I had seen her and Travis over at the bar on Jack Street."

"The Saloon?"

"Yeah, that one. They looked pretty cozy. It made me think she'd finally gotten her chance with him."

"Travis is married."

"I know. I figured that's why he never claimed Maddy as his own."

She sat back. "Did you ever ask him about it?"

"Nope." Dan took a final drag and snuffed the cigarette out on the dented metal table. "I figured if the man didn't want to have anything to do with Maddy, who was I to interfere? Vikki made her choices. Truth be told, best one she ever made was to have you be Maddy's guardian. Vikki and I...we were always kinda messed up. Even when Vikki cleaned up her life, there was the chance she'd go back to her old ways. With you, Maddy has a real shot at life."

Interesting. Grady didn't sense any deception in Dan's body language. Whether he'd known about the kidnappings or not, it seemed he was being honest about wanting Tara to have the baby.

"Other than Travis Cobb, is there anyone else who could be Maddy's father?"

"Nope."

"What about the man she told me about? The soldier who was killed in Afghanistan?"

He waved her question away. "Ten to one, Vikki made that guy up."

Tara rose from her chair. "Okay. Thanks, Dan."

He also got up. He wrapped his arms around her in a hug that set Grady on edge. Something about the way Dan looked at her...he didn't like it.

"You'll bring Maddy by to see me soon?"

"Sure." She backed away. "When all this stuff dies down, I'll bring her over."

Tara went down the porch steps, and Grady started to follow but paused. "Hey, Dan, one more thing. Where were you on Friday night around eight?"

His face hardened. "I'm a suspect?"

"Formality. I'm asking everyone."

Dan crossed his arms over his chest. "Right. Formality."

Grady waited him out. The man was on parole. He had to answer. Dan had been in the game long enough to know that.

"I was at Joe's off the highway. Went after work and was there from six onwards."

"And Saturday afternoon to evening?"

"Here." He bared his teeth. "Alone."

Grady gave a sharp nod. "Don't leave town."

"Was that necessary?" Tara demanded once they were back on the road. Darkness was starting to fall. She flipped on the headlights and angled her sedan toward the highway.

"What?"

She shot him a look. "You know what. Questioning him about where he was. Warning him not to leave town. The guy's on parole, Grady. He can't leave town, otherwise he'll go back to prison. And now he'll be less likely to give us information later."

"First of all, I'm law enforcement. Questioning suspects is what I do. I didn't grill the man, Tara, but it would be stupid of me to ignore the possibility that he's the kidnapper. Second of all, yes, it was necessary to tell him not to leave town."

"Why?"

He glanced at the side-view mirror. "Because he knew about the kidnapping attempts before you told him."

Her stomach twisted. "How do you know that?"

"His body language."

She chewed on the inside of her cheek. Grady was a human lie detector. He'd worked undercover for decades. Of course, it made sense he would see things she hadn't. But Dan? She couldn't wrap her head around the idea of him as the kidnapper.

"What's your relationship with him?"

"He's Maddy's uncle. I take her to see him once a month for a couple of hours. I'm always there with them. That's about it." She sighed. "Maybe I'm a bit protective because I see he's trying to get his life right. He started going to church. Got a job and kept it. I want him to be successful."

"I get it." His mouth twitched. "You're a do-gooder. A defender of the underdog."

She rolled her eyes. "Pot meet kettle."

"If it makes you feel better, I think Dan was sincere when he said, with you, Maddy has a shot at a good life. You were right. He did want the adoption to go through. It doesn't take him off my suspect list—hence the questions—but he isn't at the top either."

She exited the freeway and took the turn off for

Sweetgrass. It was the back way, leading through the woods and farmland, but it was the fastest route to Grady's ranch. She couldn't wait to hold Maddy again.

He twisted in his seat and looked out the back window. "You weren't overly surprised when Dan suggested Travis Cobb was Maddy's father."

"I'm surprised, but the name didn't come out of the blue. Travis repaired her car. I know she was friendly with his wife." She tapped her fingers against the steering wheel. "But he's never said more than two words to me. And he's never acknowledged Maddy."

"Sometimes that can be because a person is afraid of giving away too much." Grady glanced in the side-view mirror again. He pulled out his cell phone. "I don't want you to freak out."

"Well, the whole situation is a bit freaky—"

"No, Tara. I mean right now. I don't want you to freak out right this minute."

She tensed. "What is it?"

"We're being followed."

She glanced in the rearview mirror but didn't see anything. There were no street lights, and the road was pitch black. How did he know someone was back there?

"Just keep driving as you are," Grady said. "We're close to my ranch, so we'll go straight there."

She nodded, white knuckling the steering wheel.

Grady shot out orders on the phone. The roar of an engine came from behind. Headlights, blinding bright, suddenly illuminated the interior of the car. She spots as the glare struck off the rearview mirror straight into her eyes. The sedan jerked and Tara's head whacked against the headrest, as the vehicle behind them rammed their bumper.

Grady twisted his head and squinted at the rear window. His gun was in his hand. But how could he shoot it through the vehicles?

Tara hit the gas, trying to put some space between them and the attacker. As the speedometer climbed, she blinked in an attempt to clear her vision. A roar behind her. A new rush of light. Tara tightened her grip on the steering wheel.

"Hold on," Grady warned.

The bumper crunched and the sedan hurtled forward from the impact. Tara struggled with the wheel, forcing herself to concentrate on keeping the vehicle on the road, even as her head banged against the back of her seat. Beside her, Grady braced himself, his hand on the dash, right over the passenger-side airbag.

"Take your hand down. Take your hand down," she yelled, knowing that if they crashed, his airbag would deploy.

She weaved and swerved, making the car a harder target to hit. The truck behind them clipped the bumper once more but failed to make full contact.

"We can't outrun him," Grady yelled. "Take the turn toward the lake."

The lake on Grady's ranch. She hadn't been there in years. "I don't remember where the road is."

"Do you trust me?"

Tara yanked the wheel again, preventing the truck

from being able to strike them. She briefly met Grady's gaze. "Yes."

"Then do exactly what I say."

Swerve.

"Wait."

Weave.

"Foot off the gas, Tara."

Her vehicle barely slowed down before Grady yelled, "Now!"

Without warning, and at a ridiculously high speed, Tara took a sudden right turn toward the lake. The sedan bounced off the pavement and onto the dirt road, its tires tearing up the stones. Tara's foot struggled to find the brake. Desperately clutching the steering wheel, she tried to maintain control of the vehicle as it careened into the woods.

EIGHT

Tara's sedan looked pitiful and sad under the harsh fluo-
rescent lights of the evidence shed. The bumper was
crumpled, and tree branches had created ribbons of
scratches in the paint on both sides.

But they'd survived.

She hugged her arms around herself. Grady finished
talking with the evidence technician and ambled towards
her.

"Well, you can add stunt car driver to your list of
talents," he joked.

A laugh bubbled up her throat. "No. Never again."

After their dangerous turn into the woods, the vehicle
following them sped off. They hadn't been able to get a
license plate, although Grady agreed with her. It was a
truck.

"You did good, Tara."

Her hand flattened against his chest. His heart beat
against her palm. Solid. Steady. "I was so scared."

"I know."

She took a step forward and he pulled her close. His sports coat was soft against her cheek, and the scent of his aftershave surrounded her. For some inexplicable reason, being nestled in that cocoon unleashed the last week's pent-up emotions. Tears swept down her cheeks in rivers.

Grady let her cry, saying nothing. He simply held her. After a few minutes, she pulled herself together.

"Sorry." She sniffed, hiding her face behind a curtain of hair. There was nothing pretty about her complexion when she cried. She fumbled in her purse for a tissue. "It just all caught up with me."

"You have nothing to apologize for. You cry anytime you want. I'll provide the shoulder."

Her lips twitched. "Thanks."

His phone beeped with an incoming text. "They've picked up Travis Cobb and are bringing him down to the station for an interview. We should go."

They gave a wave to the technician photographing her car and started across the street to the police station.

"Here's the deal. We'll mark stunt driving off the bucket list. You don't ever have to do it again." He gently nudged her with his elbow. "There's plenty of other things. Skydiving. Swimming with sharks."

"Bungee jumping."

"Nope. That's where I draw the line. Tying myself to a rubber band and launching off a platform is insane."

She laughed. "Like jumping out of a perfectly good airplane is the smartest move ever."

"Do you know how many parachutes they give you?

There's backups." He held open the door to the station for her. "That bungee cord snaps and it's all over."

Tara shook her head and laughed again. The officer at the front desk waved them through, and they located Luke in the break room. A five o'clock shadow testified to his long day working on the case. The bristles outlined the scar near the corner of his mouth.

He greeted them with a lift of his Styrofoam cup. "Coffee's good."

Grady poured a cup and offered it to Tara before pouring his own. "What's the latest?"

"Travis Cobb doesn't know nothin' about nothin'. He's an upstanding citizen of the community and we have no business dragging him down to the station. I mean, *technically*, we invited him." Luke winked at Tara. "He can leave at any time but I made it clear, cooperation would go a long way."

"Is flirting just a reflex with you?" Grady pinned him with a stare. "Or do you think we could stick to the case?"

It was supposed to be a joke. Or at least, Tara thought it was supposed to be a joke. But there was a hard edge to Grady's voice that made it fall flat.

Luke grinned. "We can stick to the case. Travis claims he was at home all evening with his wife watching a movie. She confirms it. Travis drives a 2012 silver Ford F-150. There's no damage on it."

"That doesn't mean much. His wife could be lying and he's a car mechanic. He has access to other vehicles."

"Agreed." He pushed off the counter and led them

out of the break room. "We asked for permission to look around his shop, and he refused."

Grady grunted. "How surprising."

They came to an office with several monitors. Only one was lit up. On-screen, Travis sat in a room with a couple of chairs and a table bolted to the floor. His shoulder-length hair was grungy, and tattoos decorated the skin beneath his T-shirt sleeves and along the collar line. An officer watching the screen nodded at them and Tara gave him a smile.

"As far as providing alibis for the other two attacks, he used the good old 'I-don't-remember' trick." Luke rolled his eyes.

"I-don't-remember trick?" Tara asked.

"It's purposefully ambiguous but also gives him wriggle room. Once he figures out exactly what crime we're investigating him for, he will suddenly remember"—Luke used air quotes around remember—"where he was."

"And conveniently, it will be far, far away from the crime scene." Grady eyed the monitor. On-screen, Travis was drumming his fingers against the table. "He looks nervous enough."

"This isn't his first rodeo. He's trying to figure out what we've dragged him down here for. Or how much we know."

Grady nodded. He threw his cup in the trash. "Tara, you can stay here. That way you can see and hear the interview."

"Okay." She took a seat next to the officer as Grady

and Luke left. Moments later, the door to the interview room opened and they strolled in. Introductions were made—very cordial—and they went through some procedures.

After it was all done, Grady sat back in his chair. "I bet you're wondering why we asked you here."

"Kinda."

"Did you know Vikki Spencer?"

Travis's brow scrunched. "Vikki? This is about Vikki? Of course I knew her. We went to high school together. We were friends."

"Nothing more?"

His gaze darted between Luke and Grady. "Hey, is this about her murder? Because I already talked to some other detectives. I have an alibi."

"Which is what?"

"I was at a movie with some friends. Then we went to dinner."

Tara's brows lifted. Was he telling the truth? If so, it meant he hadn't killed Vikki.

"Okay. We'll look into that." Grady made a note on a pad he'd pulled from his sports coat. "So, just for the record, were you and Vikki ever romantically involved?"

Travis froze. His Adam's apple bobbed.

Grady waited him out. The silence extended until it became uncomfortable even for Tara and she wasn't the one being questioned.

"Listen, we went out a couple of times." Travis held up his palms. "But it was never anything serious. It was just a casual thing. And it was a long time ago. Long before she was shot."

"How long?"

"Uhhhhhhh, I don't know. It's been years though."

Giving him some fudging room, that meant Travis could be Maddy's father. From her position, she had a unique ability to study his features without being noticed. She didn't see anything that reminded her of Maddy.

"Can you get any more exact?" Grady asked.

"Not really. Like I said, it was a casual thing. If she was single and I was single, sometimes we went out." His smile faltered and he quickly added, "But I stopped all of that when I got married."

Travis leaned on the table and eyed Grady's book, as if he was checking to make sure the last part of his statement was taken down. "Once I tied the knot, it was all over for me. I was a one-woman man. Then Vikki got pregnant and started going to church. After that, I hardly saw her. Only if she needed her car fixed."

That didn't mean Travis wasn't Maddy's father. Vikki hadn't turned her life around until *after* she got pregnant.

Grady scribbled something in his notebook. "And when did you get married?"

"November fourth. Two years ago."

Maddy's birthday was in March so Travis had definitely been married when she was conceived. Had he killed Vikki to hide the truth? And now was he trying to kidnap Maddy to ensure his secret?

It seemed like a stretch. Plus, he had an alibi for Vikki's murder.

Grady went through forty minutes of questioning. No matter how many rounds he went, Travis insisted he and Vikki had stopped any kind of romantic relationship once he was married. Eventually, the rangers released him.

Tara waited until Travis had left the station, before exiting the observation room. Luke and Grady were in deep discussion in the hall. They stopped when she drew closer.

"What is it?"

Grady tucked his hands in his pockets. "We can't rule him out. We'll have to run down his alibi and dig more."

"But...if his alibi holds, that means he couldn't have killed Vikki. And I'm sure the other detectives checked it."

Grady opened his mouth but hesitated.

"Don't. Just spit it out, whatever it is." Tara crossed her arms over her chest. "I told you, I can't protect Maddy from what I don't understand."

"We know the gun used to shoot Vikki was also used in the attack against you. What we don't know is if the same person was holding it both times."

Her lips parted as the implication of his words hit her.

There could be two of them.

Tracking down leads. That's how Grady spent his entire Wednesday and most of Thursday but with little to show for it. Frustration and a massive headache plagued him as he crossed over the threshold of Tara's office.

The waiting room was empty of patients. Tara was talking with her receptionist/nurse. The stethoscope around her neck was decorated with a smiling worm and matched the cartoon on her scrub top. She flashed Grady a smile and his heart sputtered.

"...and that should be it." Carol picked up her purse and threw the strap over her shoulder. "I've rearranged your schedule for tomorrow. If you need to stay at home the entire day, don't worry. We can figure things out. The first priority has to be little Maddy."

"Thank you, Carol."

Grady held the door open. It earned him a smile from the older woman. "Thanks, Grady."

He made sure Carol got to her car okay before closing and locking the door. Tara was making a notation in a chart.

"Busy day?" he asked.

"It was. Cold and flu season is always rough, but there's also a bad stomach virus going around. Lots of sick kiddos." She clicked the pen closed. "I spoke with your dad about half an hour ago. He said everything is quiet."

Grady wasn't surprised Tara had been checking in on Maddy. He'd been doing the same. "The ranch is practically a fortress. Everyone, from my dad to the ranch hands, is on guard."

"I know. Trust me, it's the only reason I could come

to work these last couple of days." Tara removed her stethoscope and lab coat and hung them in a small closet. "How did things go for you? Any progress on the case?"

"Not as much as I would like." He ambled over to the waiting room chairs and started gathering discarded magazines. "Travis's alibi for the time of Vikki's murder does check out. That doesn't completely clear him, but without more evidence I can't ask for a search warrant of his shop and house. Dan's truck was also untouched."

"I told you it would be."

"I know, but we had to check. He was the last person we spoke to. It wouldn't have been difficult for him to follow us home."

"Anyone could have been lying in wait for us. There are only two roads leading to your family's property." She took the magazines from him and tucked them into the holder. "I keep mulling it over, and I can't quite figure out why he attacked us. We didn't have Maddy."

"You're assuming the perpetrator knew that. We can't even be sure he knew I was in the vehicle. Since we were driving in your car, it's possible he thought you and Maddy were alone."

Each attack was a little less planned and riskier. It upped the chances that the kidnapper would strike again. Grady knew Maddy was safe logically, but emotionally the threat weighed on him.

He rubbed his eyes. It felt like there was sandpaper inside. "The tip line we started has been getting a ton of calls. Officers are sifting through them, but it's going to take time."

She squinted. "Are you feeling okay? You look a bit flushed."

His arm was burning and had been for the whole afternoon. If he didn't do something about it, the problem would get worse. He gritted his teeth together. "Actually, there is something I need you to look at."

He unbuttoned his sleeve and lifted it up. The deep cuts ran across his skin, the area around them puffy and red.

Tara's lips pressed into a thin line. She took his hand and twisted to examine the injury in the light. The warmth of her fingers on his bare skin was far more distracting than it should've been, given the circumstances.

"This happened when you saved Maddy, didn't it?" She sighed, not waiting for his answer. "Okay, tough guy. Come with me."

She led him into an exam room and started pulling things from the cabinet above. Instead of sitting on the exam table, he opted for the chair next to the counter. No hint of bleach or antiseptic scent drifted over him. He took a deep breath. "It smells good in here. Like a garden."

"Rose and Lavender. Essential oils." She lifted his arm and spread paper towels underneath. "They're known to have a calming effect. Most people don't like going to the doctor, and I try to make the process easier. It was something I learned when my mom was sick. It didn't cure her, obviously, but natural remedies and modern medicine can work together. She loved essential oils."

She picked up a bottle and warned him. "This will sting."

"I can handle it."

She sprayed the liquid and fire burned straight up his arm. Tara leaned over. Strands of her hair had pried free of her ponytail and his fingers itched to touch them. This close to her, the faint freckles along the bridge of her nose were defined, the fullness of her lips more visible. Better to focus on her than on the injury.

"Did you know you wanted to be a doctor before your mom got cancer?"

"Mostly. I always loved biology and chemistry in school." She wiped the excess liquid from his skin. "Although I was dead set on going into oncology for a long time."

"What made you change your mind?"

She paused, her focus on his arm. Yet he sensed she was struggling with how to answer his question.

"My mom might've lived." Her voice trembled. "If there had been a doctor in town back then, if she'd caught the cancer earlier, she would've had a fighting chance."

Her words hit him like a gut punch. His breath caught. "I didn't know that."

"No one does. I found out after I went to medical school. That's when I decided to come back to Sweetgrass."

To be their doctor and prevent others from suffering the way her mother had. The way she had. He'd known some of her reasoning had to relate back to her mother's illness, but hearing it from her own mouth moved him more than he expected.

"Your mom would be proud. Not just because you became a doctor or for moving back here, but also for adopting Maddy. None of those things were easy."

Tara shrugged. "She raised me to be tough."

Yes, she had. Vulnerability wasn't something Tara revealed often, yet here she was, showing it to him. She trusted him. To protect her and Maddy. To cry on his shoulder. To tell him things she didn't share with others.

It was the wall. The one he'd sensed was always there and couldn't figure out how to traverse. She was taking it down. Coupled with her recent touches, the way she looked at him...maybe there was something more between them than just friendship after all.

He swallowed hard. Grady had faced down hardened criminals and terrifying drug lords without batting an eyelash, but the idea of sharing his feelings with Tara left him queasy.

Being honest with her might take more courage than he had.

NINE

Tara had dressed wounds hundreds of times. She'd always been able to focus on the task at hand, but with Grady, it was nearly impossible. He smelled like hay and sunshine. His skin was bronzed from working outside, the muscles of his forearm strong and well-defined.

"I'm almost done." She opened the overhead cabinet and snagged an extra tube of antibiotic ointment. "I'll give you this to take home. You need to use it twice a day and change the bandage."

"Okay." He shifted in the chair and cleared his throat. "Do you have any advice for my leg? I've done everything the doctors have told me, but it aches and I get cramps."

The admission couldn't have been an easy one. Grady was a proud man. A slow warmth spread in her chest. She was touched he trusted her enough to ask.

"There are some stretches I can show you. Big ones for when you are at home, but even smaller ones you can do in the car or while at the office. It'll prevent the muscles from becoming stiff, which should reduce the cramps."

The need to keep their relationship light, for her own self-preservation, meant she avoided asking Grady deep questions. But this time, she couldn't help herself. "What was it like? Working undercover."

"An adrenaline rush. Like riding a rollercoaster without the seat belt." He half shrugged. "It's not for everyone. You have to stay cool under pressure and lie with ease. Plus the risks are high. If the information you have is bad or if a confidential informant betrays you, things can go south fast."

"Is that what happened to you?"

He hesitated, and she wanted to kick herself. Asking for help with his leg didn't mean he wanted to discuss how the injury happened. She focused on cutting a bandage. "Never mind. We don't have to talk about it."

"No, it's okay."

Her hands stilled.

"We got some reliable information about a gambling ring that moved from place to place to avoid detection." The words came out slowly, painfully. As if he were removing porcupine quills one at a time from bruised and tender flesh. "The operators of the ring had multiple streams of income—not only gambling but also drugs. An undercover officer with the local police department had received a tip about the next location. It was decided the two of us would go in together along with his confidential informant. We'd verify the leaders were in-house and then bust the entire group. For this type of operation, backup is down the street and we wear cameras and microphones. At first, things went as planned, but something about the confidential informant felt off to me. I worked my rescue signal into a sentence—"

She frowned, and he caught the expression.

"It's a word you give when everything goes south. In my case, it was karma. It signals to law enforcement in the truck to move in." His jaw tightened. "Backup couldn't get to us fast enough to stop the ambush."

She sucked in a sharp breath. "Your instincts were right."

"Unfortunately. They saved my life, but the other officer died." He stared at the tile floor, his voice hollow. "Max Walker. I didn't know him well, but it doesn't matter. He was one of us."

"I'm sorry." She reached out and grabbed his hand. "It's a weak phrase that doesn't help much, but it's the truth. I wish things had gone differently."

"So do I."

The pad of his thumb brushed against her knuckle. Heat coursed up her arm.

"I struggled for a while afterward." He kept his attention locked on their joined hands. "Guilt can do a number on you. Getting shot also made me realize I wasn't invincible."

Is that what had brought on this attraction? She'd always known Grady was good-looking. There was never a doubt about that. But the wisdom in his eyes was new.

There was a depth to him, an understanding that hadn't been there when he was younger.

"It changed you."

"It forced me to figure out what I really want. I love law enforcement. It gives me purpose, but it's not everything." He met her gaze. Held it. "I want to share my life with someone. Raise my children on the ranch that has been in our family for six generations. Be part of a community."

His words tugged on a place inside of her she'd buried and hadn't wanted to acknowledge. She also longed for a sense of home and belonging. She hadn't had anything close to it since her mom died.

Grady rose and Tara didn't move. The air between them shifted, electrified. She licked her lips. "Why...why haven't you dated since moving back?"

"I've been holding out for someone special, but I'm not sure how she'll react if I tell her the truth." Grady reached up. His fingers brushed against her hair, tucking the loose strands behind her ear. "I don't want to scare her off."

Her breath hitched. Her. He was talking about her. The thrumming of her heart increased. She leaned closer. His gaze dropped to her mouth.

Yes.

The thought was instinctive. Not fully realized or even one she could question. Grady tilted down, sweeping his lips against hers. The kiss was light. Butterfly soft. He backed away slightly, questions and concerns etched into his features.

Tara closed the distance.

The moment their lips touched, sparks flew. Grady's arms came around her and drew her closer. Everything dropped away. There was nothing but him. Them. These feelings swirling inside of her and the sensation of his mouth on hers.

She didn't want it to end.

A cell phone trilled, bringing her back to reality. Grady groaned and rested his forehead against hers. "Sorry. That's me."

Tara's brain jumped to worst-case scenarios. "Maddy."

"No. My parents have a special ringtone." He released her and pulled the phone from his pocket. "West."

Luke's voice filtered out of the speaker. Grady squeezed her arm and mouthed witness.

She nodded. Taking her own cell phone from her pocket, she shot off a message to Grady's mom. A reply came back almost immediately. Maddy was having a snack. Accompanying the text was a photo of her daughter wearing a wide smile and a giant-sized bib.

Tara touched a finger to her lips, still warm from Grady's kiss. What was she doing? Playing with fire, that's what.

Grady hung up, and she showed him the photograph. He smiled. "She's having the time of her life."

"She's a foodie, that's why." She clicked her phone closed. "What's up?"

"A witness has come forward who thinks he saw the

perpetrator on the night of your attack. He called into the station after seeing it on the news. I'm going to talk with him, but I can drop you off first."

"No need. I'll go with you. Maddy's fine and I wanted to stop by my house and pick up clean clothes for the next couple of days anyway." She removed the back of the bandage and pressed the edges against his skin. "Okay, you're good to go. I want to check it tomorrow evening and make sure it's healing well."

"Tara..."

She shook her head. "Let's not talk about it now. We're fine. I promise. There's just a lot going on."

"You're right." He scraped a hand through his hair. "It's just...I don't regret it. I hope you don't either."

The thread of uncertainty in his voice tugged at her heartstrings, slipping right past all those defenses she couldn't manage to keep up around him anymore.

"No. I don't regret it."

His mouth quirked at the corners and she found herself smiling back. His phone beeped with an incoming message. He glanced at it. "Luke sent me the address. And a name. Jason Gonzalez."

She froze. "The artist?"

"Yes. Luke mentioned something about that. Why? Do you know him?"

"No, but Vikki did."

Grady was a man of action.

He knew how to take charge of a situation. He also prided himself on being able to read people. There was a time to push and a time to hold back.

It was definitely time to hold back with Tara.

He'd dumped a lot on her lap in the last half hour, plus what she was already dealing with. The timing was awful, and Grady had little doubt Tara's romantic feelings toward him were new. She would need time to sort them out. He would wait.

And he would continue to be here. For her and Maddy.

"Did Luke say when Jason called into the station?" Tara asked, cutting into his thoughts.

"Sunday afternoon." Grady slowed his truck at a red stoplight. "Was there any relationship between Jason and Vikki? Beyond the professional, I mean."

"Not that I know of. She didn't say much about him, only that his artwork was very good and he seemed like a nice guy. Truthfully, I wouldn't have remembered the conversation except there aren't that many professional artists out this way. It piqued my interest." She paused. "Then again, Grady, it's possible she knew him better than I understood. Vikki didn't tell me everything."

It was something that had been bothering him. "How is that possible? She felt comfortable enough to make you the guardian of her baby."

"The guardianship came as a surprise to me. We'd had a passing conversation about it, but I never thought she'd hire a lawyer and move forward with the paperwork." She reached up to play with her cross necklace. "Although, in hindsight, I should have realized how serious she was. Vikki had lost her parents in a car accident and their deaths affected her. She didn't have many friends, and Dan couldn't be relied on. She was alone with Maddy. Honestly, she reminded me of my own mother. Trying to do the right thing for her baby and working hard to make that happen. I felt for her and tried to help out as much as I could."

"But you weren't close?"

"We were. Or...I thought we were. Dan mentioned once Vikki looked up to me, almost like I was an older sister."

Grady grunted. "Which means she cared deeply about what you thought and filtered what she told you."

"Based on what I've discovered since her death, I think so."

That left a lot of wriggle room. "Maybe this Jason guy can give us some answers."

The GPS led them to a strip mall near the county line. Jason's studio was tucked between a laundromat and a barber shop. The tinted windows made it impossible to see inside. Grady pulled on the door handle. Locked. Cupping his hands over his eyes, he peered in. Easels with canvases of different sizes were placed around the room. A few sculptures. A bare desk in the rear. No computer. No phone.

"It doesn't look like anyone's here," Tara said.

"Hey, dude, what are you doing?"

Grady turned. A man wearing a black apron glared at

them. The barber's shoulders were thrown back, his stance wide, as if he was spoiling for a fight.

He frowned. "Mack?"

The other man's posture relaxed. "Grady. I didn't recognize you. Long time, no see."

At least a decade. Mack had been a freshman player on the football team in Grady's senior year. His athletic form had softened around the edges, but his hands, capable of cradling a football the way most men did a lemon, were still the same. Huge.

Mack's gaze shifted to Tara. She stepped around Grady to extend her hand. "Tara Sims."

"You're the doctor in Sweetgrass, right? My aunt Bessie says you're the best doctor in three counties." He turned back to Grady. "What are y'all doing?"

"We're looking for Jason Gonzalez. Any idea when he'll be back?"

"No. Why? He in trouble or something?"

"Not at all. I'm hoping he might be able to help me out on a case." Grady parted his jacket enough to flash the badge pinned to his shirt. "I'm with the Texas Rangers now."

"I heard that rumor. Some of my clients come from Sweetgrass, and they keep me apprised of the comings and goings."

Grady tossed a thumb over his shoulder at the studio. "When's the last time you heard from Jason?"

"Couple of days ago. On Monday, I found a note slipped under my door telling me he was going on vacation. He didn't say where, but he asked me to keep an eye on the place for him."

Grady frowned. Jason took off right after calling in to the tip line. A sinking feeling started in the pit of his stomach. "Do you still have the note?"

"Naw. I threw it away." Mack scratched his chin. "You know he was military?"

Tara's shoulders stiffened. Grady shook his head.

"Yeah. Got the scars and stuff from being blown up. Anyway, Jason always takes a vacation about this time of year. Something about the anniversary of the attack. Last year, he was hiking out in West Texas."

"Do you happen to have a contact number for him? The one he gave is for the studio."

Mack frowned. "Jason doesn't have a cell. But he generally calls in every couple of days to check on things."

"When he does"—Grady pulled out a business card —"can you ask him to contact me?"

"Absolutely."

They chatted a bit more. Before leaving, Grady stopped and slid another business card under Jason's door.

"Is it always like this?" Tara asked when they got back into the truck. "Phone calls and chasing people around?"

"Yeah. And paperwork. Lots and lots of paperwork." He pulled out of the lot. "But it's all necessary. Cases can be busted wide-open by paying attention to the details."

"One thing Mack said caught my attention."

"The fact that Jason was in the military."

"Yeah." She fiddled with the air vent. "Vikki mentioned Maddy's father was a soldier. Maybe it's Jason. Or someone Jason knows."

"Could be. It's an avenue worth pursuing." He turned a corner onto the street running behind the strip mall. They'd arrived from the other direction, and he wanted to get a feel for the area since he didn't come out this way often.

Tara frowned. She pointed to the faded sign above a commercial garage. "Isn't that Travis Cobb's shop?"

With a jolt, he realized she was right.

A chain fence enclosed the back half of the property. Grass and weeds tangled with wrecked cars and stacked tires. Grady slowed down. The bay doors to the shop were open, but no one was visible. Still, a prickly sense of unease made him regret bringing Tara.

He sped up.

In the rearview mirror a man appeared, watching them go.

TEN

Tara hauled the suitcase off the bed. Hopefully, she'd packed far more than she needed. She loved staying with Grady's parents and being on the ranch made her feel exponentially safer, but catching the kidnapper would be even better.

She wheeled the bag to the top of the stairs. Below, Grady waited next to the newel post. Their eyes met and she stumbled. She grabbed onto the railing to stop from falling.

He took the stairs two at a time and intercepted her, taking the suitcase from her hand. "Got everything you need?"

Her gaze dropped to his mouth. The memory of their kiss invaded her thoughts and a heat flushed her cheeks. Tara gave herself a mental shake. Now was not the time to deal with anything more than keeping Maddy safe.

"For at least a week. Sorry about this. When I packed the first time, I hadn't expected to stay at the ranch for so long." She followed him down the stairs, ignoring the way his sports coat emphasized his broad shoulders. "Did I hear you talking to someone on the phone?"

"Luke. He's still running down leads, but I asked him to push Jason Gonzalez to the top of the list. We have a BOLO—a Be-On-The-Lookout—on his vehicle. We're going to talk to Jason's neighbors as well as any family he has. I'm hoping someone knows more about his where-abouts. I don't like the fact that all Mack had was a note. Especially given the timing."

Her brow wrinkled. "Are you thinking he's on the run?"

"Could be. I don't want to rule anything out." He held the front door open for her. "The detectives have sent over Vikki's entire file, including their interviews. I'm going to look through as much as I can tonight. Maybe we'll find something there."

The clouds hung low overhead, the sky dark and threatening. The wind chimes on Tara's porch danced. She shivered and hunched down into her coat.

Grady used his body to block her from the wind as she locked up. "Rumor has it, Mom is making lasagna for dinner."

"That sounds amazing." Her stomach fluttered as he placed a hand on the small of her back to guide her down the walk. "I missed lunch because I was trying to squeeze in as many patients as necessary—"

Her steps faltered. Leaves scattered across Vikki's yard and a squirrel jumped into her oak tree. Tara smacked her forehead with her hand.

"Grady, I need to go back inside and get the keys to Vikki's house. A neighbor mentioned that he spotted a hole in one of the eaves and some squirrels might've moved into the attic. I meant to check it earlier but completely forgot."

"Okay." He opened the truck and stowed her suitcase in the back seat. "Let's move quick, though. The storm is coming in fast."

Tara raced into the house and fished the keys out of her kitchen drawer. When she came back outside, Grady was standing next to the truck with a hefty flashlight. He clicked it on and the beam cut through the night. Together, they crossed the street.

"Do you know where the hole is?"

"Has to be on the right-hand side." She pointed to the house next to Vikki's. "Ken was doing work on his own roof when he spotted it."

The grass sank under her steps. She led Grady to the fence and unlocked the deadbolt. He directed the flashlight on the eave, and it wasn't long before the beam cut across a chunk of missing wood.

"Oh, no." Tara stood on her tiptoes to get a better look. "That's big enough a squirrel could get inside. What a mess."

Grady frowned, his flashlight beam tracing the hole. She turned and hurried to the back door. A bolt of lightning lit up the sky. It shimmered across a gap between the door and the frame. Tara froze.

"Grady," she whispered.

His head snapped in her direction. Her fingers tightened around the keys, the edges biting into the soft palm of her hand. "The door isn't locked."

Her words were like a blast of icy wind. Grady closed the distance between them in three strides. Keeping his eye on the door, he placed himself in a protective position in front of Tara. He used the flashlight to scan the yard and the back of the house. No windows were broken. The door jamb didn't appear damaged.

"Who else has keys to the house?" he asked.

"No one. At least, no one is supposed to." She swallowed hard. "Of course, it's possible someone else does. I didn't change the locks after Vikki died."

Grady drew his weapon, but hesitated at the threshold. What to do with Tara? He didn't want her returning to her house alone. Nor did he want to leave her outside in the yard by herself. There was only one other option left.

"Stay right behind me. Keep your hand on my belt and don't let go."

She nodded. He edged the back door open wider with his foot. The kitchen was stripped bare, the flowered wallpaper faded. His boots made no sound on the linoleum. His gun was pointed at the floor, his finger next to the trigger. The last thing he wanted to do was shoot someone who legitimately had access to the house. Behind him, Tara's breathing was rapid.

As quickly as possible, he cleared the living room and

half bath. Every room was devoid of furniture, making the process much easier. Together, silently, they moved toward the bedrooms. Only two. The door on the right was open. He rushed inside.

No one. The accompanying bathroom door was cocked open. Grady approached at an angle. Pushed it with the toe of his boot. Also empty.

Lightning cracked. Tara jumped.

He turned and leaned down, right next to the shell of her ear. "There's just the last bedroom. Take my flashlight. After I turn the knob, I want you to give it back to me. Then you stay outside the room until I tell you otherwise."

She swallowed hard but nodded. She was a champion. Grady was trained for this. She wasn't. Keeping cool under this situation took a strong will and a level head.

He handed her the flashlight. Her jaw tightened. Tara might not have a weapon, but he had no doubt she had his back. He crept into the hall. This was the most dangerous of all. If someone was inside, had they heard Grady and Tara moving through the house? It was possible.

He twisted the knob, careful to keep Tara and himself clear of the door. It cracked open. He reached behind him, and she slid the flashlight into his palm. He took a deep breath. Tara released her hold on his belt.

Grady bolted into the room in one stride.

His gaze swept over it, his mind processing the sleeping bag on the floor, the ashtray, and the discarded food wrappers in quick snaps. The bathroom door was open. No one was inside. He immediately moved to the walk-in closet.

Empty.

He holstered his gun. "It's clear. There's no one here now."

Tara moved toward the items on the floor.

"Don't touch anything," he ordered. "It's evidence."

The sleeping bag was crumpled and open. Grady bent down next to the ashtray. It was full of discarded butts, but the room didn't stink of smoke. Whoever was squatting in Vikki's house hadn't been here recently.

"What's that on the windowsill?" Tara asked.

Grady lifted his flashlight. The beam hit on a set of high-powered binoculars. Fat raindrops smacked against the window pane, drawing his attention to what was beyond.

Tara's house.

He reached for her, instinctively wanting to protect her from what he'd figured out, but he was too late.

Tara gasped. Her hand flew to her mouth, and she took a step backward.

"Someone's been watching us."

Grady didn't feel fear often. At least, not that he registered anymore. His work undercover forced him to bury his emotions to get the job done. Being a ranger wasn't much different. Yet the feeling plaguing him, as he walked from his home to his parents' across the ranch, could only be described as fear. Not for himself.

For Tara. For Maddy.

He had to get a grip on it. He couldn't allow emotions to cloud his judgment so last night, after making sure the ranch was secure, he'd pored over Vikki's murder file. His eyes needed toothpicks to hold them up, but the hard work had paid off. He'd found something worth digging into.

He stepped onto the porch and wiped his boots on the mat before entering the mud room and hanging his hat on the hook. A flash of color caught his eye. Tara and Maddy were in the kitchen. The baby was dressed in footed pajamas, her rebellious curls wild. She rested her head against her mother's shoulder. Tara rocked side-to-side and whispered words to Maddy, the soft murmur of her voice drifting across the room.

A warmth radiated through his chest. He was a plumb fool. There was no way he could separate his emotions from this case. When it came to Tara and her little girl, things were too complicated for that. The feelings he had for them were instinctive. Fiercely protective. Deeper than anything he'd felt before.

Tara glanced up and her eyes brightened. "Good morning."

"Morning. Did you sleep well?"

"No." Her hand traced a path down Maddy's back. "This little one has a tooth coming in. She was up and down."

Tara had shadows under her eyes. Her hair had been

pulled back, but she was still in her pajamas. Grady wrapped an arm around her and pulled her next to him. She sighed, leaning on his shoulder.

Words didn't need to be said. It was enough to just hold them.

Maddy's head poked up from Tara's shoulder like a turtle coming out of its shell. Poor thing looked awful. She had her fingers in her mouth and her nose was running.

Grady held out his hands. "Hey there, darlin'. How about we give your mama a break?"

The baby leaned over, and he lifted her. The sweet scents of baby powder and clean laundry detergent wafted over him. Tara grabbed a tissue off the counter and swiped it under Maddy's nose.

"I've given her some pain medication and rubbed numbing cream on her gums, but this tooth is proving to be a tough one." She sighed again. "There's a fresh pot of coffee. Would you like some?"

"I'll get it. Sit before you fall down."

"No." She rubbed a hand over her face. "I probably look bad, but I've done long nights before. Medical school was a test of endurance. How about we divide and conquer? You hold Maddy and I'll start breakfast."

"Somehow, I got the better end of the bargain."

She smiled softly. "There is something about holding a baby, isn't there? Even if she's snotty and cranky."

There was. In fact, it was downright amazing. Maddy laid her little head on his chest and his heart squeezed so tight, he thought it would burst.

Tara opened the fridge and eyed the ingredients. "How about an omelet?"

"You don't even need to ask. The answer to that question is always yes." He retrieved some mugs from the cabinet, being careful not to jostle Maddy. The coffee was strong and dark, just the way he liked it. "Mom and Dad still sleeping?"

"Your mom is out in the barn taking care of the horses, but your dad's still asleep." She cracked an egg into a mixing bowl. "I think he's sleep-deprived. I've heard him making rounds every night since we got here."

Keeping watch. There was an alarm system on the house, but his dad wouldn't count on it alone. Grady understood. He'd been making his own rounds at night.

"I feel bad," Tara continued. "I hate putting your family in this position."

"You didn't do anything. The only person to blame is the monster doing this. Besides, my dad would lose a whole lot more sleep worrying about you and Maddy if you weren't here where he can keep you safe. He cares about you. We all do."

She took a deep breath and let it out slowly. "You have a way of putting things in a whole new perspective and making me feel better."

"Good."

He cupped her face, brushed his thumb against the curve of her cheek. Their gazes met. Held. His pulse kicked higher.

Tara's focus shifted to his lips. "If you keep distracting me, I'm going to burn your omelet."

"It'll be worth it."

He tilted his head down and captured her mouth with his. She leaned into him, bringing her body closer. Her lips were soft and he lingered, relishing the stolen moment, pouring all of the emotions he couldn't put into words in his kiss.

Something wet and slimy touched his neck. He broke the embrace, his nose wrinkling. "I think she oozed me."

Tara laughed. She ripped off a few paper towels and handed them over. "Sorry."

"I've been covered in worse." He wiped Maddy's chin before mopping the spit up from his neck. "Try to keep it in the tummy, kid."

She blinked at him. Her eyes were glazed and red. Poor thing really didn't feel good. He kissed her forehead. "Tara, do you need to go into the office today?"

"No. Carol is amazing. After I called last night, she managed to reach everyone who had an appointment. Thankfully, most of them were routine issues we can put off for a few days. If anyone has anything urgent, they can call my cell."

The scent of sizzling bacon filled the kitchen. Grady's stomach growled. "If we need, we can make house calls. I'll go with you."

"Thanks. We'll play it by ear and see how it goes. Right now, I want to put as much energy as possible into catching this guy." Her hand tightened on the spatula, the knuckles turning white. "Last night proved to me he isn't going to go away."

Grady had come to the same conclusion. "I had a

forensic team out to Vikki's house. They didn't find fingerprints, but we might get DNA from the cigarettes."

The problem was DNA took time. And they needed something to match it to. If they were lucky, the guy was already in the system. Maddy shifted against him. The baby had fallen asleep, her long lashes casting shadows on her cheeks.

I'm gonna get him, baby girl. I'm not going to let anything happen to you or your momma.

"What can we do in the meantime?" Tara asked. "What about talking to Vikki's other friends?"

"Officers are going through the list you gave. However, I want to talk to your next-door neighbor Ken Hastings."

"Ken?" Tara slid the omelet onto a plate and divided it into two. She added bacon and toast. "Why?"

"I came across his interview in Vikki's file. Apparently, he went to high school with her."

"That's not surprising. They are about the same age and Sweetgrass only has one high school."

She reached out to take his hand and bowed her head. Grady blessed their food. He used his fork to cut the omelet. Taste exploded in his mouth. Cheese, peppers, and tomatoes.

"This is fantastic." He cut another piece. "What was Vikki and Ken's relationship like?"

She lifted a shoulder. "They used to go out sometimes, but Vikki told me it was just as friends. She liked him, but I don't think there was anything romantic between them."

"What about Ken?"

"I know he cared about her. Whatever was going on between them, there wasn't any bad blood. Why?"

"Ken told the detectives there was trouble between Vikki and her brother. He specifically said they should take a hard look at Dan."

Her mouth popped open. "He's never said anything to me. I know he isn't fond of Dan, but...I told him about the reward I'd put up for any information into Vikki's murder. He knows I was determined to get to the truth. Why wouldn't he have told me about his suspicions?"

"That's a good question." Grady's hand tightened around the fork. "And it's one we should ask."

ELEVEN

Grady took a chance, hoping Ken would be at home, and was rewarded when the front door swung open revealing a man in his late twenties wearing sweatpants and a Patriots T-shirt. His face was clean-shaven and angular with a large nose. Ken's attention landed on Tara and his eyes lit up behind his glasses.

"Hey, Tara. How are you? I knocked on your door the other day, but you didn't answer. I heard about Maddy. Is everything okay?"

"Maddy's fine, thank goodness. I haven't been at home much. I'm staying with friends."

Grady stepped forward to shake the other man's hand. "Texas Ranger Grady West. Do you mind if we come in and talk to you?"

Concern flickered across the other man's expression, but he didn't hesitate to open the door wider. "Of course not. Although I should warn you, I have to get to work soon."

"We'll try and keep it short."

The house was a two-story, modeled after Tara's own with an open floor plan. A book on cybersecurity sat on the coffee table next to an empty plate with a few crumbs, and a comedy re-run played on the flat-screen television.

Ken picked up the remote, and clicked the TV off. "What has my brother done this time?"

"What makes you think this has anything to do with your brother?"

He snorted. "When doesn't it? Wayne's been in and out of jail since he was seventeen- years-old. He's caused enough trouble for ten lifetimes."

"It's not about Wayne," Tara assured him. "It's about Vikki."

Ken let out a breath and his shoulders dropped. "Oh. Well, that's a relief."

He seemed to realize the reaction was a touch dismissive because he quickly added, "Sorry, that came out wrong. It's just I've gotten so used to police showing up on my doorstep because of Wayne." Ken gestured to the couch. "Take a seat. Can I get you anything to drink? Coffee?"

"Nothing for me, thanks," Grady said.

"Me either. Thank you for the offer," Tara said.

Grady removed his hat and gestured toward the book. "You like cybersecurity?"

"I'm a Security Specialist for Freeman so I work hard to keep up on the latest vulnerabilities."

Freeman Security provided everything from home

alarm systems to cybersecurity programs. Grady joined Tara on the couch. "Do you like it?"

"They pay well, which is important. My mom has diabetes and my brother isn't any help. Keeping up with her medical bills isn't easy." Ken folded his frame into the recliner and swiveled to face the couch. "I don't know how much I can help you with Vikki's murder. I've already told the other detectives everything I know."

"We're just making sure nothing has been missed. As I understand it, you knew Vikki for a long time."

"Kinda..." He pushed his glasses further up on his nose. "We went to high school together, but it wasn't until she moved in next door that we became friends."

"Did she ever mention any trouble to you? Anything that was bothering her?"

Grady purposefully left out the information he already knew. He wanted to see how much of Ken's statement would match the previous one he'd given to the detectives shortly after Vikki's murder.

The other man hesitated. He let out a breath. "She was having issues with her brother, Dan. He was constantly after her for money. She gave him some for a while, but it never seemed to end. Dan's had a problem with gambling as well as drugs. He stole stuff from their parents and, after they died, blew through his inheritance. That's when he started getting arrested for breaking and entering."

"She never mentioned any of this to me," Tara said.

"No, Vikki was private about it. She probably wouldn't have told me either except we were at the movies one night when Dan confronted her. He wanted money, and she refused to give it to him. The conversation got heated before he drove off. Vikki started crying. I comforted her and we got to talking about our brothers. I think it made her feel better to know she wasn't the only one with a screwed-up family."

"How long ago was this confrontation?" Grady asked.

"It was right after he got out of prison, about a year before her death. Vikki wanted Dan to turn his life around. She convinced him to go to church and the pastor talked with him. After that, she said their relationship got a lot better."

"But you still think Dan had something to do with her murder?"

Ken held up his hands. "I didn't say that exactly. I told the detectives it was an avenue to pursue. Listen, addicts have a habit of falling off the wagon. Even if things between Dan and Vikki were fine, it was always possible they could take a turn for the worse."

True enough. Grady made a mental note to reach out to his counterparts. He knew first-hand illegal gambling rings were hard to track. Even if Dan hadn't been arrested at one, it didn't mean he wasn't using them.

"If you thought Dan might be responsible, why didn't you say anything to me?" Tara asked.

His brow wrinkled. "Because I told the detectives. I assumed they would pursue the lead, and when nothing happened, I figured I was wrong. Are you telling me they didn't?"

"No, they did," Grady said. "Again, we're just trying to ensure nothing was missed."

"I'm sorry, Tara. Maybe I should have said something, but I didn't want to smear his name. Sweetgrass is a small town and rumors can run wild. Goodness knows, I've been on the wrong end of a few with Wayne's criminal history."

His reasoning made sense. Grady could understand why he would hesitate to share the information. Everything Ken had said so far tracked with the statement he'd given to police earlier. But there were a few new questions Grady needed to ask.

"Did you and Vikki ever date?"

"We went out as friends but nothing more than that." He sighed. "Between work and my mom, I don't have the time for relationships."

"Did Vikki ever talk about Travis Cobb?"

Ken's mouth tightened. "I warned her away from him. The guy is bad news. He's been arrested a few times, and he's married. The last thing Vikki needed was to get involved with a married man."

There was something in Ken's tone. A protectiveness. Had he been jealous of Travis? Maybe. Or maybe it was exactly as he said. He didn't want Vikki to make a bad decision.

"What about Maddy's father?" Tara asked. "Did Vikki ever talk about him?"

"It was some guy she'd met. A soldier."

Grady leaned forward. "She ever mention his name?"

"No. Like I said, Vikki was private." Ken checked the

watch on his wrist. "Listen, I hate to do this, but I have to finish getting ready for work. I don't want to be late."

"Of course." Grady rose and pulled out a business card. "If you think of anything else, even if it's small, give me a call."

"I will."

He escorted them to the door and opened it. Grady paused. "Hey, Ken, one more thing. Have you noticed anyone hanging around Vikki's house? Since her death, I mean."

"Yeah. I've seen Dan coming and going from time to time." His brow furrowed. "He has a key. Vikki gave it to him."

Tara wiped a drop of milk from the bottom of Maddy's lip and laid her in the crib. The baby sighed, tossing her hands over her head. They drifted to the mattress as she settled in. The nightlight caressed her face.

Tara's heart squeezed. Maddy was so small and defenseless. They were making headway on the case, but every step forward created more questions than answers. She bent over and kissed Maddy's forehead before raising the crib's side. She grabbed the baby monitor, taking it with her from the room.

A tea kettle whistled. Her feet made no sound against the tile floor, but still Grady turned as she entered the kitchen. The corners of his mouth lifted in a smile that didn't quite manage to reach his eyes. "Maddy sleeping?"

"Finally. Where is everyone?"

"Mom and Dad went to bed. Janet had work in the morning, so she left a while ago." He removed the kettle from the stove. "I dug around inside the cabinets and scrounged up some tea. It's not green, though. And I don't have cookies."

A lump formed in the middle of her throat at his thoughtfulness. "Never mind. Your mom made enough food for an army. I might not eat until next week."

"Crisis management West-style. Problems are a lot easier to solve when your belly is full of fried chicken and apple pie."

She chuckled. "Mind if we walk outside a little? It would be nice to work off a bit of this meal before I sleep." Tara lifted the baby monitor. "This reaches all the way to the fence line, and I'll have some tea when we get back."

"Sure thing."

She grabbed a light jacket and they went outside. The brisk air was scented with the faint smell of woodsmoke and grass. Tara took several deep breaths. Her shoulders relaxed. Overhead, stars sprinkled across the night sky.

"Gosh, it's beautiful here. Hard to believe there's more rain predicted tonight with the sky so clear." She tucked her hands in her pockets. She dreaded opening the conversation, but delaying wasn't going to make it any easier. "I've been thinking a lot about what Ken told us today, but I can't make heads or tails of it. I have a hard time believing Dan is behind all of this. Honestly, I can't figure out what motive he would have to kill Vikki and then months later try to kidnap Maddy. None of it makes sense."

"How many people knew about the guardianship arrangement?"

His question threw her. She blinked. "The lawyer did, but I'm not sure about anyone else. I didn't even know."

"I contacted our Criminal Division. Dan's name has been linked with a gambling ring running in the area. There's no proof, just rumors, but it confirms what Ken told us." They reached the fence line, and Grady leaned against it. "I suspect Dan didn't know you were made Maddy's guardian. Without those papers, he would've been her next of kin."

"You think he murdered his sister in cold blood because he wanted her money? Vikki didn't have any."

"She had more than Dan. Ken told us he confronted her at the movies. Maybe he lured her to that country road to ask for money. When she refused, he shot her."

"But he didn't rob her. Her cell phone and purse were still in the vehicle."

"Too easy to trace. Dan's been arrested for burglary several times. He knows how the game is played. He wouldn't have risked it. We may have been approaching this from the wrong angle. We assumed ransom wasn't the motive because Maddy didn't inherit any money. But you're her mother now. How much would you pay to get her back?"

Tara stepped away from him. She didn't need to answer. He already knew.

Everything. She would give everything she had to get Maddy back.

She shook her head. Logically, she was following him, but emotionally...Tara wasn't ready to go down that road. "Dan's impulsive. I can't believe he would have the discipline to pull this off."

"He may have learned his lesson from his previous crimes. Criminals in jail talk. Teach each other things. We shouldn't underestimate him. I think Dan's a lot smarter than people give him credit for."

"Where did he get the truck? The one that ran us off the road? The police looked at his, and it didn't have a scratch on it."

"Travis. They're friends. It could explain why Travis was worried when we pulled him in for questioning and why he refused to let us inspect his shop." Grady sighed. "There's something else, Tara. Officers went out to Dan's house to bring him in for questioning. They couldn't find him. His truck was missing, and he hasn't been to work in three days."

She hugged herself. The swirling emotions were hard to decipher. Inexplicably, tears welled, making the stretch of land beyond the fence blur.

"I'm sorry," Grady whispered. "I don't want to cause you more pain."

"It's not your fault. I don't know why I'm so upset."

His hands clasped her shoulders. "Because you can't stand the thought of someone you know doing this."

No. She couldn't. Especially Maddy's uncle.

Grady's gaze met hers. The moonlight caressed his features, casting them in a pale blue glow. His jaw was scruffy with whiskers. She raised her hand and cupped his face. Her thumb traced the curve of his jaw, lightly skipping over the scrape on his skin.

His fingers encircled her forearm, drawing her closer, until their mouths met.

The kiss heated her from the inside out. This man was a mass of contradictions. He threw himself in front of trucks to save children and rumbled with some of the roughest criminals in Texas, but he could also be tender and gentle. One hand pressed against her back. The other cradled her head. She felt feminine in his arms. Desired. He touched her like she was everything he needed.

It made her want. Want for things she wasn't sure were even possible. Or smart. Tara broke the kiss and dropped her head to his chest. "What are we doing? Grady, I don't want to ruin our friendship or mess up my relationship with your family."

"Let's get one thing straight right now. We will always be friends. As far as my family goes, no one knows about us and that's exactly how it can stay if you don't want to take things any further."

"That all sounds good, Grady, but it isn't realistic. You know. I know. It changes things."

"Sweetheart, I've been hiding my feelings for you for the last eight months. I've gotten pretty good at it."

"You—" She pulled back to look him in the face. "Are you serious? Why didn't you say anything?"

"Because you're not the only one who's worried about affecting our friendship."

"And now, what? You aren't worried."

"I am."

His hand brushed a strand of hair off her face. A trail of heat followed his touch.

"But seeing you and Maddy in danger...Tara, it changes things for me. I'm done putting off things that need to be said. This isn't a one-off. Or a crush. I'm crazy about you. I'm pretty sure I'm falling in love with you."

Her heart stuttered and then jumped into overdrive. The image of her father, carrying his suitcase out the door, flashed in her mind. She swallowed hard. "I come as a package deal."

"You think I don't know that? I don't just want you, Tara. I want Maddy too. She slipped in when I wasn't looking and stole my heart."

"It's risky. It could all fall apart."

It had for her mother. They'd had a family, a child. Her father had still left. Love didn't always bind people together and not every couple weathered the storm.

Grady tilted her chin up until she was looking him in the eyes. "I'm willing to accept the risk. Tara, you're worth it. The real question is: are you willing to do the same?"

TWELVE

Everyone always underestimated him.

He dropped the shovel. Rain spattered him, running down the brim of his hat and into his shirt collar. His breath came in shallow spurts.

He shoved on the fence post. Dark thoughts, of murder and pain, clouded his mind. Vikki's face flashed in front of his eyes—her mouth open in shock, blood spreading across her T-shirt. An incredible rush of power fueled his straining muscles. He shoved harder.

The wood gave way. It collapsed into the mud, yanking the barbed wire down with it.

He smiled. Soon he would have everything he wanted.

Maddy.

Tara dead.

This time, failure wasn't an option.

It was all or nothing.

THIRTEEN

When Tara woke up on Saturday morning, bright sunlight streamed in through the curtains. She rose and checked on Maddy. The little girl was sleeping on her back, the blanket kicked off and in a heap at the bottom of her crib. Tara touched her forehead. No fever but the poor thing had to be exhausted. She covered her with the blanket and left her to rest.

Downstairs, through the french doors off the living room, she caught sight of Deeann. Grady's mother was on the wraparound porch, her scrapbook open on the table. More wedding stuff, no doubt.

"Good morning," Deeann greeted her with a smile. Her sable-brown hair was gathered at the nape of her neck, and she wore a beautiful sweater to ward off the chill in the air. In the distance, Raymond was repairing a section of the barn.

"Morning. Actually, it's nearly afternoon. I don't think I've slept this late in years."

"Well, it's no wonder with the schedule you've been keeping and the stress you've been under. Working with Grady during the day, up half the night with the baby. How is Maddy?"

Tara settled into one of the cushion-covered chairs. The cell phone in her sweater's pocket stabbed her in the ribs. She adjusted it within the zippered pouch to a more comfortable position.

"Still sleeping." She set the baby monitor on the table. "I think the tooth finally broke through so she should be feeling better today after some good rest."

Deeann poured a cup of coffee from a carafe on the table and handed it to Tara. "You just missed Grady. He left about an hour ago."

"I know. He messaged me."

The warrant to search Dan's home had come through. Grady and Luke were overseeing it. Tara wasn't sure how to feel. Uncovering evidence would mean Dan was the kidnapper. It would provide answers and, once they found him, eliminate the threat. At the same time, he was Maddy's uncle. Family. As silly as it might sound, Tara wanted him to be innocent.

Deeann suddenly jumped up. "What's going on?"

Across the yard, Raymond was running in their direction. Tara rose.

"The storm knocked out the back fence." His words came in a rush. "The cows are loose and so are some of the horses. Where's Grady?"

"He's gone." Tara didn't hesitate. "Go. We'll lock the doors and set the alarm. We'll be fine."

The cattle were the same as cash. The horses even more valuable. They would need every hand possible to round them up before they were hurt. Raymond hesitated but then nodded. "Do it. I'll wait."

The women went inside and Tara punched in the code. The alarm panel glowed green. Raymond took off toward the barn and his horse.

"I hope they're able to get them all," Tara said.

"Me too." Deeann clutched the scrapbook to her chest. "How about some food before the baby wakes up and we're running after her? I'd love your opinion on some of the wedding options, too."

A distraction, one her racing heart could use. "Sure."

Thirty minutes later, Tara turned the last page in the scrapbook. "I don't think there's a bad choice in here. You have lovely taste."

"Thank you, dear. Just make sure you remember that when the time comes to plan your wedding." Deeann's lips twitched and she wagged her finger. "You're getting the same treatment for your own big day."

The sentiment caused Tara's breakfast to harden in her stomach. She glanced at the book of wedding ideas. "Sorry to disappoint but I'm not sure marriage is in the cards for me."

"Why not?"

"It didn't work out so well for my parents."

Grady's words from their conversation last night echoed in her mind. She bit her lip. "Love requires a leap of faith, and I don't know if I have it in me."

Deeann reached out and grabbed her hand. "Of

course you do. Look at Maddy. Choosing to become her mother on your own took a huge leap of faith."

"Not really. Vikki named me and Maddy needed someone. It was the right thing to do."

"But you could have refused. You didn't. How did you know which decision to make?"

She let out a breath. "I let my heart guide me."

"So you did. You've faced difficult challenges since taking on the responsibility, but you never gave up. You dug in your heels. Falling in love and getting married, it's the same."

"But, Deeann, so many couples don't make it. Like my mom and dad. How do you know your marriage will?"

"You can mitigate it by picking someone who matches your goals and dreams. Someone who loves you as much as you love them. But, ultimately, there are no guarantees. That's why it requires a leap of faith. Most things worth having in life do."

She leaned back in her chair and sighed. "I don't think that helped me."

"Well, maybe this will. Trust yourself, hon. God will guide you, but you have to listen to your heart and not your fears." Deeann patted her hand and rose from the chair. "I'd better get started on the laundry. There's a pile of dirty clothes so big, I could get lost in them."

She walked out, leaving Tara in the comforting silence of the kitchen. Sunlight streamed in through the windows and played with the wood grain on the table. The scent of coffee lingered. There were dishes to be done and Maddy would wake soon, but Tara didn't move from her spot.

She was lost and Deeann was right. God could only guide her if she listened. She bowed her head.

Lord, I've been spending a lot of our conversations talking about keeping Maddy safe, but there's something else I'm struggling with.

The words flowed out of her, and when she was done, the answer in her heart was undeniable.

She was in love with Grady.

Logically, she'd known he was steadfast. He'd proven able and willing to keep her and Maddy physically safe from harm. But trusting him with her heart, letting him see every part of her, was terrifying. And yet, what she hadn't wanted to acknowledge or face was that the same fears she had, he shared. The fear of failing. The risk of losing their friendship. Of messing up things for her and his family. He held back his feelings, not because he wasn't ready to share them, but because she wasn't ready to receive them.

Grady thought of her. Every step of the way.

He was nothing like her father. Not even close. When times got hard, he didn't shy away. He faced it head on. But she realized her issue had never been with Grady.

It had been with herself.

Deep inside, she'd always wondered and worried, when push came to shove and things got hard, would she stick it out like her mother? Or bail like her father? Adopting Maddy—and dealing with the threats—proved she had what it took to ride out the hard times. She wasn't a quitter. Her father had given up on his family. She fought for hers.

She was her mother's daughter. Tough. Resilient. Strong. A woman of faith.

She'd let her fears get in the way, but that was coming to a stop right now. The life she desperately wanted was within reach, and Tara was going to grab hold and never let go—

A crash came from the back of the house accompanied by a thump. Her pulse jumped. What was that? Silence followed.

Tara rose from the chair. "Deeann?"

She passed the stairs and went into the back hall. The laundry room was empty and the washing machine lid stood open.

"Deeann? Are you okay?" She entered the master bedroom. A pair of stocking feet stuck out from the other side of the bed. Tara raced over. Her shoe collided with a perfume bottle, sending it sailing across the room.

Deeann lay facedown on the carpet. Her vanity chair was tipped over, the silver tray holding her perfumes next to her. Several bottles were scattered about.

"Deeann!" Tara leaned down and pressed her fingers to the woman's neck. A pulse. She scanned her but didn't see any obvious reason for her to be on the floor. Gently, she turned her over. Blood soaked the carpet and a huge gash marred the area around Deeann's temple.

Tara's gaze lifted to the vanity. Had she fallen and hit her head on the edge?

She blinked. There was no blood on the corner. There was no blood anywhere other than on Deeann and the carpet.

Her heart galloped as her attention shot to the french doors leading out to the porch. The alarm panel was dark.

Maddy!

Tara bolted up. She grabbed the shotgun from the mantel above the small fireplace in the corner of the bedroom. Popping it open, she checked to make sure there were shells inside. Raymond had taught her how to shoot long ago, a skill she'd never hoped to use, but was now glad she had.

Her feet whispered against the carpet. Keeping the shotgun at the ready, she climbed the stairs. If the kidnapper was in the house, Maddy was his target. She would not let him take her baby.

Blood roared in her ears. The urge to close the gap between her and her daughter was overwhelming, yet Tara slowed her steps. She took a page from Grady's book and cleared each room as she passed it. Her bedroom was at the end of the hall. If someone was in there, they would have to go through her to get down the stairs.

The bathroom was first. Biting back her fear, she pivoted into it.

Empty.

Sliding sideways, she scooted up next to the other bedroom and looked inside. Also empty. That left only her room.

Holding the shotgun firm against her shoulder, she listened. Nothing. The tick of the grandfather clock was extraordinarily loud. So was her breathing. If someone was back there, he was keeping quiet. Her stomach clenched and sweat dripped down her back.

She crept forward, keeping her finger next to the trigger. The bedroom door was cocked open, exactly as she'd left it. The crib came into view, Maddy's sleeping form visible through the slats. Tara quickly closed the distance to the doorway. Her breath came out in a whoosh.

The room was empty.

She lowered the shotgun. Her legs trembled. They weren't out of danger yet. She needed to get Maddy out of the house. She started toward the crib—

The creak of the door behind her registered too late. She whirled. A crack reverberated through her skull. She crashed to the floor, the shotgun falling from her numb fingers. Stars clouded her vision.

Something sharp jabbed her neck.

Everything went black.

"We've got him." Luke's voice came over the speaker in Grady's truck. "Hidden in the back of Dan's closet was a clown costume, complete with a red wig, and the same type of ammunition used to kill Vikki."

Grady's vehicle bounced over ruts in the dirt road. "The net is getting tighter. We need to find him."

"Every lawman in the state is looking for him. I'm also giving his photo to the media and naming him as a person of interest. You get anything from Jason Gonzales?"

"Not yet." He pulled to a stop in front of a hunting cabin. The area was north of Huntsville and popular during deer season. "I just got here. If he can help us identify Dan, it'll add to the mounting evidence."

"Agreed. Good luck. Call me when you're done."

The air smelled of pine and wet leaves. The rain from the last two days had left the ground soggy and moist. Mud clung to his boots. Grady knocked on the faded wooden door of the cabin.

No answer.

He knocked again, this time with more force. No sound came from inside. He leaned over and peered through the curtains. The furniture was rustic, the space one big room divided into separate areas. No one appeared to be inside.

Where was Jason? He knew Grady was coming. They'd talked on the phone earlier.

Unsnapping the button on his holster, he kept his hand on the butt of the gun and went around the side of the house.

A growl stopped him in his tracks. A huge shepherd mix stood in his path, teeth bared, the hair standing up on the back of its neck. Grady pointed his weapon at the dog. He didn't want to shoot him but would if he had to.

"Connor, heel," a voice commanded from the porch.

The dog turned. A scar cut through the animal's fur extending down his left side. Connor raced to his owner standing in the shadows.

"Ranger West?"

Grady kept his weapon trained at the ground but still ready. "Yes."

The man stepped into the light. He wore cargo pants, a long-sleeved shirt, and combat boots. Scars crisscrossed his left cheek, extending down into his collar and outward toward hair the color of midnight.

"Jason Gonzalez."

He extended a hand, also covered in scars. Grady holstered his weapon and shook it.

"Sorry about the dog. I can't hear well out of my left ear so he acts as my alert system."

Connor watched them with laser-like precision from his place on the porch. Grady had the faintest impression if he made one wrong move, the dog would attack.

He kept his hand on the butt of his weapon. "Understandable. I'd like to talk with you about your call into the tip line."

"I figured as much when Mack said you'd stopped by looking for me." Jason straightened his posture. "Listen, like I told the officer on the phone, I didn't realize the significance of what I'd seen until later."

"What did you see?"

"I was across the street from Burks at the pharmacy. This guy drives up in a truck. An old clunky Ford. That's what made me notice him. You don't see many of those trucks around anymore, and it was clear he'd changed out the engine, souped it up to run fast. Anyway, he gets out and he's wearing all black. Instead of going to the pharmacy, he heads toward the grocery store. As he's crossing the street, he pulls a black cap out of his pocket and puts it on."

"Did he cover his face?"

"Are you kidding?" Jason's mouth twisted. "If he'd covered his face, I would've followed him after calling the cops. No, he covered his hair with it. But after I heard the news reports, I figured the two could be connected."

Smart. "If you saw the man again, would you be able to identify him?"

"Absolutely."

"We have a suspect, so I'd like you to view a photo array for me."

"No need." Jason turned and gestured for Grady to follow him. He opened the back door of the cabin, the dog at his heels, and went inside. He picked up a drawing pad from the table. "I sketched him for you."

He flipped to one of the pages and set it down. "That's him."

Grady stepped closer. His brow furrowed. "Are you sure this is the guy you saw in the parking lot that night?"

"Positive. I'm an artist with a photographic memory. I don't forget faces." Jason frowned. "I take it this isn't your suspect."

"No, it isn't." His jaw tightened. "But I recognize him."

FOURTEEN

Maddy was crying.

Tara groaned. Her head was splitting apart. She tried to move her arms but couldn't. The crying got louder, stabbing at her head and her heart. She pried her eyes open. The light pierced straight into them and she winced. What was wrong with her?

"I said, wake up!"

A slap of something wet slammed into Tara. She sputtered and opened her eyes again. Soaked hair hung in her face. Beyond the strands were a pair of men's shoes. A bucket hit the wooden floor with a clank. Memories rushed into her mind.

Deeann on the floor. The shotgun. Maddy.

Her heart thundered. She lifted her gaze to the face of her captor. Ken. Her next-door neighbor. Her body shook, as much from the shock and terror as from the icy water dripping down her skin.

Ken bent and picked up Maddy from the dirty floor.

The little girl was frantic, twisting, red with the effort of her cries. She reached out her chubby hands in Tara's direction.

Don't. The word reverberated in her head like a scream. She tried to get her mouth to work but couldn't. The room spun. Whatever drug he'd given her hadn't worn off.

"What is wrong with her?" he demanded. "She's been crying for half an hour and won't stop."

"Give—" The word came out on a croak. Her mouth was dry. She licked some of the water off her lips. "Give her to me."

Tara fought against the bonds holding her to the chair. The ropes bit into the delicate skin of her wrists.

"I'm not giving her to you. You're going to tell me what to do."

Was he insane? "Ken, please let me go. She's scared."

"She's not scared!" he shouted. His face became mottled with rage. "I just don't know what to do. You're supposed to tell me what to do!"

His outburst terrified Maddy. The little girl arched away from him. He barely caught her before she hit the floor.

"Okay. Okay, I'll tell you what to do." Tara didn't understand everything that was going on, but one thing was very clear: she needed to keep Ken calm. "Rock her. Side to side. She likes that."

She took several deep breaths, hoping lots of oxygen would clear the fog from her brain. Her gaze swept across the room. They were in some kind of cabin. Through the windows, she could see towering pine trees. Near the front door sat Maddy's diaper bag.

"She's teething, so her mouth may be hurting. In the bag, I have ointment for it."

Ken crossed the room and bent down. "Where?"

"In the front, left-hand pocket. You have to smear it on her gums."

Someone groaned. Tara twisted her head, pushing past the sharp arc of pain. Dan sat in the corner of the room. He was unconscious and dressed in his work uniform. Dried blood stained the collar and matted in his hair. One of his eyes was black, and his shoulder jutted up in an unnatural position.

Maddy's cries lessened as Ken spread the numbing medication. She started hiccupping, her face still red, her eyes swollen. Tara wanted nothing more than to scoop her up and run.

She had to get them out of here.

Ken smirked. "See. I knew she wasn't scared. You tried to trick me, but I'm not an idiot."

"I don't think you're an idiot." She had to keep him calm. She also had to keep him occupied. *Lord help me find the words.* Tara twisted her fingers, feeling for the knots binding her wrists. "I just don't understand why you are doing this."

"Because Maddy is mine."

No. He couldn't be her father!

Don't think about it. Get free. Get Maddy. Get out.

"But I don't know how to take care of her," he continued. "That's why you're here. You're going to tell me everything I need to know." He sneered with disgust. "If Vikki hadn't been so foolish, we could've been together. We could've been a family."

Her hands stilled. "You...you killed Vikki? *Why?*"

"She rejected me."

Ken's expression twisted into one Tara had never seen before. It was hard. Ugly.

Evil.

"I loved her. Since high school, I've loved her. When she moved in next door, it was fate. We started dating. Movies. Dinners. It was beautiful. Vikki told me she only wanted to be friends, but I knew it wasn't true. She was mine. She just needed more time to realize it. After she became pregnant with Maddy, I told her it didn't matter. I would marry her. I offered her everything. Everything! And she said no."

Maddy jerked and started crying again. Tara's heart shredded with every tear. "You can't use a loud voice. It's jarring. Walk with her. She's exhausted, and if you walk and rock her, she'll fall asleep."

Ken sucked in a deep breath. He awkwardly patted Maddy's back. "There now, my baby. No one could keep us apart in the end. No, no. You're mine. You're the best part of Vikki and now you'll be with me forever."

Tara's stomach twisted in disgust. Ken's obsession with Vikki had turned into something dark and perverse and, after killing her, he'd become fixated on Maddy.

The baby quieted, and he tossed Tara a smile. "I knew taking you was smart. I've read baby books and I've watched you for a long time, but there's so much about

Maddy I still don't know. What other things can I do to calm her down?"

"She likes listening to people talk. It's soothing."

If Ken needed to learn how to care for Maddy, then she would use that to her advantage. The rough rope tore at the skin of her fingers, but one of the knots yielded. Tara wanted to cry with relief. Instead, she said, "Were you the one who attacked me in the grocery store parking lot?"

"Did you honestly think it was *Dan*? Of course, I've worked hard to point the police in his direction." He snorted. "Cops. They're just like sheep. Plant some evidence, give a witness statement, and they follow it right where you want them to go."

Plant evidence? The ropes loosened but not enough. She tugged her hands apart. The twine cut deeper into her skin and warmth trickled down.

"You put things in Dan's house?"

"The clown costume. Some bullets. Just enough to make him look guilty." Ken glowered at her. "If you hadn't fought me that night in the parking lot, none of this would have been necessary. You screwed it up for me."

She wasn't sorry she'd fought back, but Tara regretted her actions drew Dan into it. "You tried to kidnap Maddy from the bridal store."

"That was a setup. In order for it to be believable Dan was the kidnapper, he had to appear desperate." Maddy's head drifted down onto Ken's shoulder. He kept walking. "But I was never desperate. I knew exactly what I was doing."

Tara's fingers, slick with blood, slipped off the rope. *Please, Lord, help me.*

"What about the truck that followed us?"

"I stole it from Travis's garage. He and my brother, Wayne, go way back. Birds of a feather and all that. Again, it made the kidnapper look out of control." He sneered. "I led you to Vikki's house because I needed you to believe Dan was watching you. I took cigarettes from his ashtray and planted them. DNA doesn't lie. Between what they've found in Vikki's house and the evidence I planted in Dan's closet, the case will be rock solid against him."

She fumbled with another knot. Her fingers wouldn't coordinate, the effects of the drug working against her. If she could only loosen it...

"The break-in at the West's house was more planned."

A smile broke across his face. "You bet it was. It took a bit of time, because I had to figure out how to get all of the men away from the house. I needed the storm to cover my trail when I knocked down the fence to let the cows out. Then I watched and waited."

"How did you bypass the security system?"

"Which company do you think put it in? The people at work have no idea how vulnerable their systems are."

The cybersecurity book on his coffee table. He'd hacked into the system at work and obtained the alarm codes.

"And the drug you used on me?"

He chuckled. "My brother. Having a drug dealer comes in handy sometimes. He supplied me with enough to keep Dan in line. Plus some for you and Deeann too. I was a bit worried when Grady's mother made all that noise when she fell, but it worked in my favor. I knew exactly where you would go once you realized someone was in the house."

He'd used her love of Maddy against her. Tara tightened her jaw and kept working the knots.

"She's asleep." Ken gently laid Maddy into the car seat he must have taken from the West's home. He covered her with a blanket. "All right. Now it's your turn."

He picked up a pad and paper from the table. "I want to know everything. From the moment she gets up to the second she goes to sleep—"

A cell phone rang. Tara's fingers froze as she realized it was coming from her sweater. "You have a cell phone on you." His face turned beet-red, and he jerked the zipper to her pocket open. Curse words flew out of his mouth. "You stupid—"

His hand smashed into her face, cutting off the rest of his sentence. Tara's head snapped back as pain exploded across her cheek. The edges of her vision darkened. She forced herself to breathe through the agony.

"It's Grady." Ken's steps pounded against the cabin floor as he paced. He cursed again. "They can track you using cell phones. What am I going to do? What am I going to do?"

He reached behind his back and yanked out a thick blade with a serrated edge. Tara's mouth went dry. "Ken—"

"Shut up," he screamed. He lifted the sleeve of his shirt. Along his forearm, lines of cuts ran back and forth. He lowered the knife and sliced his skin, slowly and with exact precision. His eyes closed and his breathing slowed.

Her phone stopped ringing.

"I should destroy it." He lifted the blade. Blood ran down his arm and coated his hand. "That will prevent them from being able to track it."

No! He couldn't destroy it. That phone represented her lifeline to help. The cell phone's screen lit up moments before the ringing started again.

"Let me talk to him."

He glared at her. "What kind of fool do you take me for?"

"Grady will keep calling. If I don't talk to him, he'll immediately know something is wrong."

Ken's mouth flattened into a hard line. He flicked his wrist. The knife whizzed past her ear and embedded in the wood behind her. She gasped. The handle was even with her face. One centimeter over and it would have cut her.

He closed the distance between them with angry strides and yanked the knife from the wall. She froze. The blade's edge caressed her cheek and then the line of her jaw. It hovered over her carotid artery.

"Okay, Tara. I'll let you talk to Grady, but if you breathe one word to him about what's happening I'll kill

Maddy's loving uncle right in front of you. I'll send this knife straight into his throat."

She locked her muscles and willed herself to meet his gaze. His eyes were dark voids of emptiness.

"Deal." Her voice didn't tremble with the lie, even as her mind raced. "I won't say anything."

How was she going to tell Grady they were in trouble without tipping off Ken?

Grady hit redial on his phone. This was his third time calling Tara. Two sets of eyes—Jason's and the dog's—watched as he paced the cabin. He'd already talked with Luke, and sent him a photograph of Jason's drawing identifying Ken Hastings as the man who attacked Tara in the parking lot. Still, he wouldn't be content until he was able to alert her.

"Hello."

He let out the breath he'd been holding in a rush. "Tara, where are you? Why didn't you answer the phone?"

"I was changing Maddy's diaper. Hoy, boy, it was a doozie. Karma really got me on that one. I shouldn't have fed her those beans yesterday."

Grady froze. His throat tightened to the point of nearly closing. Somehow he managed to choke out, "Better you than me."

She laughed, but it was strained. "Chicken. Anyway, everything's okay here. Any news on your end?"

"No. Nothing." He let frustration color his tone. "We've hit a bunch of dead ends."

"You'll get there. I'd better run. Maddy needs to go down for her nap."

"Other than the beans situation, she okay?"

"She's fine. We both are. I'll see you when you get home."

Before he could answer, Tara hung up. Grady immediately called Luke. "Get someone out to my parents' house."

The urgency in his voice caused the dog's ears to stand up. Over the line, Luke snapped out orders and said, "What's going on?"

Keeping his fellow ranger on speaker, Grady toggled to view his apps. "Tara's in trouble. I just talked to her on the phone and she used my old undercover rescue word."

Karma. Using it had saved his life, but it hadn't spared the officer he'd been with. The idea of Tara or Maddy being hurt or killed sent a wave of heart-stopping panic rushing over him. "I think Maddy's with her. She said they were fine, but she could've been lying."

"Maddy?" Jason grabbed his arm. "As in Maddy Spencer?"

"You know her?"

"She's the daughter of one of my combat buddies. Marcus died in an IED attack. The woman robbed in the parking lot of Burks was Maddy's adoptive mother?"

Grady nodded. A map appeared on his cell phone screen. A blue dot blinked. "I've got the phone's coordinates, Luke. Tara gave me permission to track her phone after Maddy was kidnapped at the bridal store. I'm sending them to you right now."

"I grew up around here and know these woods." Jason leaned over to look at the phone. "There's a cabin there."

"We've been running Ken Hastings through the system since you sent me the drawing," Luke added. "His mother owns a piece of property in that area. I've got law enforcement dispatched to that location, but they are thirty minutes out."

"I know a shortcut. We can be there in fifteen, less if you're a fast runner."

Grady hesitated. Jason was a former marine with several medals to his name, but he obviously knew Maddy and he'd known Vikki. Could he be trusted?

"You've done a background check on me. I've never had so much as a traffic ticket." Jason's mouth tightened. He lifted his shirt to reveal a sidearm. "That's my buddy's daughter in there. You need backup and I can provide it."

Grady was going with his gut. "Done. Let's go."

FIFTEEN

Tara talked until her hoarse throat nearly gave out.

"She likes colorful toys...her favorite lullaby is...she hates bananas."

Blood dripped down her fingers as she worked the last knot, one stubborn tangle of rope in her way. Her hand cramped, and she stole precious moments to stretch it out.

Ken stood from the chair and yawned. He tucked the pen and pad into his pocket. "I think I have enough. None of this seems too complicated."

"But I haven't told you about when she's sick."

"And I wish we had more time, but it's getting late. Someone is eventually going to find Grady's mother and realize you're gone. Once that happens, they'll track your phone." His gaze flickered over the room. "My grandfather left me this place. I'm going to be sorry to see it go."

Ken ambled over to the only closet and opened it, then removed a huge can.

Tara sucked in a sharp breath. "What...what are you doing?"

He tipped the can over. The scent of gasoline filled the space.

"I'm finishing what I started."

Grady's bum leg burned, but he didn't slow down. Ahead of him, the dog—Connor—jumped over a log. He followed suit, and his boots slipped on the mud and pine needles. His shirt was soaked in sweat he barely noticed. His mind had one focus: getting to Tara and Maddy.

Please, Lord. Please don't let me be too late.

Jason skidded to a sudden halt, his chest heaving, and winced. Grady probably wasn't the only one in pain.

"The house is in a small clearing through those trees." He crouched behind some bushes, and Grady joined him. "We've got the high ground, so we should be able to assess the situation before going in."

A hundred yards away sat a cabin with a tin roof. Windows faced the front and side. There was no cover between them and the house. Anyone standing guard would see them coming.

He texted Luke. The response came right back.

"Backup is here in fifteen," he whispered.

"We hang tight till then?"

It went against Grady's instincts. He wanted to rush the house and get Tara and Maddy out of there, but without knowing more, he could just as well kill them.

"If we try and approach now, we could create a hostage situation." He pointed to the truck next to the cabin. "Is that the vehicle you saw on the night of the attack?"

Jason nodded.

The door to the cabin opened and Ken appeared, carrying a car seat. Maddy was tucked inside, her curly hair bouncing with his steps. Grady's hands clenched into fists. He was going to make sure Ken spent the rest of his life in a prison cell.

He set the baby down in the yard and went back inside.

"What's he doing?" Jason whispered.

Grady rose. He didn't like this. Assessment time was over.

"Get the baby," he ordered. "I'll get Tara."

He streaked across the clearing, his weapon in his hand. Footsteps behind him meant Jason was following suit.

A scream rang out inside the cabin.

Tara.

No, no, no. The word pounded in his head as his boots tore up the distance between him and the cabin. Jason scooped up the car seat and ran toward the trees. The dog trailed behind him.

Grady shoved on the wooden door, but it didn't budge. He lifted his foot and slammed his boot into the wood right above the lock. Red-hot pain shot up his thigh.

"Tara!" he screamed.

He reared back and repeated the movement. This

time the wood splintered and the door burst open. Grady bolted in, his gun raised.

And froze.

Ken stood in the back of the cabin. He held Tara in front of him. His arm wrapped around her waist and trapped hers next to her body. Her face was pale, her hands raw and bleeding. Rope dangled from one wrist. A long cut ripped through her right pant leg. Blood soaked the fabric.

Ken held a knife to her throat.

"Put down your weapon, Ranger, or I'll slit her throat."

His voice was silky soft. Menacing. Ken was cornered, and like any cornered animal, he was at his most deadly.

Sweat dripped down the back of Grady's neck. His boot slid across the floor as the urge to rush over and tear Ken limb from limb wrestled with his law enforcement training. "No one needs to die today."

Tara's mouth moved, but Grady couldn't make out the word. A moan came from the corner of the room. Dan was tied to a chair, unconscious and beaten. The scent of gasoline burned his nose. With a jolt, Grady realized what word Tara was mouthing.

Fire.

"It's over, Ken. Don't make things worse than they already are." Grady calculated the shot. He couldn't make it without risking Tara. "We can all walk out of here."

"You mean I can go to prison. That's not going to happen. Put your gun down now, or I'll cut her carotid. I know exactly where it is. Do you hear me?" Ken's face heated with rage. He dug the edge of the blade into Tara's neck. Blood beaded. "I'll finish her."

His hand trembled, and he tightened his hold on the weapon. Grady couldn't lay his gun down. If he did, Ken would just kill him and then Tara.

"Ken, listen to me, we can work something out. You don't want to do this."

A shadow moved outside the window. Grady's attention shifted for half a heartbeat. Something flew from Ken's hand. Flames shot up. Within seconds, the entire back wall of the cabin was engulfed.

"The clock is ticking, Ranger. Once the fire reaches the gas can, it's over." Ken's mouth twisted into a sick smile. "We all go boom."

Grady met Tara's eyes. She looked down and then back at him. She did it again. Smoke made the room hazy.

Ken laughed. "Now, what's it going to be? Ready to put down—"

Tara maneuvered one hand out of Ken's grasp and slammed her elbow into his stomach. He grunted, the blade lifting from her throat, and Tara dropped like a rock to the floor.

Grady fired.

The bullets slammed into Ken's chest. Blooms of red appeared. He stumbled back and collapsed to the ground, his body going limp.

Grady closed the distance. He kicked Ken's knife away before crouching next to Tara. "Are you okay?"

"Dan. We need to get Dan out."

She grabbed Ken's knife and crawled over to the injured man. Dan moaned.

"Get out of here." Grady took the blade from her and sliced at the ties binding the other man to the chair. "Go, Tara. Get out."

"Not without you."

She tore at the ropes. They were a mess. Dan was secured several times over. The fire spread, the cabin going up like a matchstick. Within seconds, the entire perimeter was ablaze. Grady lifted Dan into a fireman's hold. Smoke burned his eyes and lungs. Tara started across the room but stumbled and hit the cabin floor.

Her leg. She couldn't make it, and Grady couldn't save them both.

Water splashed in from the doorway. The fire retreated, and like an answer to Grady's unspoken prayer, Jason appeared. He threw the empty bucket to the side. "Give him to me and get her."

The marine buckled under Dan's weight but recovered and disappeared into the smoke. Grady bent and scooped Tara into his arms. Her blood coated his hand, warm and slick. It pumped out of her with every heartbeat.

"Grady..."

"Stay with me, Tara." He raced for the door. "I need you."

He couldn't lose her. He wouldn't.

Fresh air caressed his face just before a loud explosion roared behind him. Heat seared his back as he slammed into the ground. He rolled, protecting Tara's body with his own, wrapping her in his arms.

All around them shards of wood and ash fell.

SIXTEEN

One month later

"It was, by far, one of the best weddings I've ever been to," Tara declared. "Janet, you looked perfect in your gown. The food was amazing, and the ceremony at the church couldn't have been any lovelier."

"It was better because you, Grady, and Maddy were all there to see it," Deeann announced. "I know I've said it a hundred times, but don't scare me like that again."

A chorus of agreement rose from the table. The entire West family had gathered for a celebratory lunch the day after the wedding. Janet and Todd were heading off for their honeymoon in a few hours. Lauren, Grady's other sister, and her family were flying back to Nashville tomorrow.

Maddy banged her hand on the table and Lauren's two-year-old twins followed suit.

Grady waved his finger between them. "I can see these three are going to be trouble."

His tone was full of affection and it warmed Tara's heart. After the attack in the cabin she'd been at the hospital and then stayed on the West's ranch, recuperating. Ken had sliced her deeply when she'd tackled him after removing her bonds. It'd taken surgery and physical therapy to put her back together.

Grady had been there every step of the way. He'd helped with Maddy, brought Tara books and magazines, and taken her to the doctor's appointments. They'd had conversations and even a stolen kiss or two. However, between Janet's wedding and a houseful of guests, there hadn't been a lot of private time with Grady to discuss their future.

Now the wedding was over. Tara was fully healed. Maddy was safe. Tomorrow, things would go back to normal. Then, Tara vowed, she would tell Grady everything she was feeling.

"Who wants more roast beef?" Deeann asked, lifting the platter. Most of the table groaned.

"I don't think I could eat another bite," Janet declared. "It was amazing, Mom."

"Well, I hope you saved room for dessert. I have three kinds of pie."

Tara checked her watch. "Deeann, if you don't mind, Jason and Dan are stopping by in a little while. I'd love to have them join us for dessert."

"Absolutely. How are those two?"

"Good. Jason's asked to spend some time with

Maddy, and I've agreed. Marcus was an orphan, and Jason is the closest thing he had to a brother. I think it'll be good for Maddy to have someone in her life who knew her father."

"Well, Jason has proved himself worthy as far as I'm concerned," Deeann said. Grady's mother had already made the marine an honorary member of the family. "And Dan?"

"He's fully recovered from his injuries and back at work. He even signed up for a course at the community college. I think Vikki would've been really proud of him."

Tara had a pang of sadness thinking of her friend. A journal found in Ken's house after his death documented his obsession with Vikki. Her refusal to marry him was the final straw. He lured her out to the country road under false pretenses and killed her.

Afterward, as Tara had surmised in the cabin, Ken's fixation turned to Maddy. In his twisted thinking, taking her would enable him to possess Vikki. He'd created an elaborate plan to keep Maddy in secret until he could move to another state.

Tara thanked the Lord every day that they'd been able to stop him. However, Vikki's death haunted her. It was a tragic end for the young mother who had finally found her way in life. Tara was determined to share the truth with Maddy when she was old enough to understand. Vikki had loved her with everything she had.

As if he could hear her thoughts, Grady reached under the table and squeezed her hand.

"Well, if everyone is finished, I guess that's my cue."

Raymond pushed his chair back from the table. "Deeann does the cookin' and I do the dishes."

"That's cuz no one wants to eat your cooking, Dad," Grady joked.

Everyone laughed. Tara helped clear the table. Maddy strained in her seat and managed to grab some mashed potatoes off a nearby plate left too close. She banged it on the high chair tray table, sending food remnants flying.

Janet tossed Tara a clean washcloth. "That's all you, Mama."

She rolled her eyes. "Thanks."

Tara wiped Maddy's hands and face. "You are a mess, baby. What am I going to do with you?"

Her little girl grinned, revealing four baby teeth. Tara dropped a kiss on her head as she removed the oversized bib. Underneath, Maddy's pacifier string was attached to her dress. The baby tugged on it.

"Where did this come from?" Tara said, taking it gently from the small hand. "You haven't used your pacifier—"

Her fingers stumbled across the end. She glanced down at her hand. Instead of finding the pacifier, there was a diamond ring.

Tara's mouth dropped open.

A familiar hand came into view, unclipping the string from Maddy's dress. "I know we haven't been dating long, but we have known each other our whole lives, so I figure that should count for something."

Grady lowered himself to one knee in front of her.

143

Behind him, his whole family stood. Tears blurred her vision.

"Tara, there isn't anything about you I don't adore. You're kind, you're brave, you can take down killers with your sharp elbows."

She laughed. Maddy banged on her tray table and screeched. Grady kissed one of her plump hands and ruffled her hair. "Hold on there, kid, I'm trying to convince your mom to marry me."

"She doesn't need any convincing." Tara swiped at the tears running down her face. "The answer is yes. Yes, I'll marry you."

The room erupted into cheers. With a slightly shaky hand, in front of all the people they both loved, Grady slipped the ring on her finger before rising from his knee. His mouth brushed against hers. Sweet, tender, and full of promise.

"I love you, Tara."

Warmth spread through her. "I love you too."

Grady released her and scooped Maddy up in his arms. "Hear that, darlin'? We're going to be a family."

The little girl laughed. Tara wrapped her arms around them both. She leaned into them. Leaned into the love.

She'd found home.

ACKNOWLEDGMENTS

First, I must thank the Lord for putting this novel in my heart and urging me to write it. I once heard a story that God sends you a hint in the form of a whispers. If you don't listen, He sends a pebble and then a bolder. Let's just say, I nearly needed a mountain slide before finally heeding the call. Amazing things have opened up in my life since then, and I'm extremely grateful.

Additionally, I cannot move on without giving a huge thank you to my family. They sacrificed, in big and small ways, and none of this would've been possible without their support.

Texas Rangers are an invaluable law enforcement branch of Texas, but they are also an iconic part of the state's history. This book would not have been possible without the help of Byron Johnson, Director of the Texas Ranger Hall of Fame and Museum. He patiently answered my questions, and his guidance was invaluable.

Some aspects of the novel had to be adjusted for fiction. All of the mistakes are my own.

To my editors, critique partners, and beta readers, your hard work and comments made all of the difference. This book is better because of you. Thank you.

ALSO BY LYNN SHANNON

Available Now

Vanish

Ranger Protection

Ranger Redemption

Ranger Courage

Coming 2020

Ranger Faith

Would you like to know when my next book is released? Or when my novels go on sale? It's easy. Subscribe to my newsletter at www.lynnshannon.com and all of the info will come straight to your inbox!

Reviews help readers find books. Please consider leaving a review at your favorite place of purchase or anywhere you discover new books. Thank you.

Made in the USA
Monee, IL
12 May 2020